the Angels' Share

Also by Robert Irvine

Baptism for the Dead
Ratings are Murder
Footsteps
The Devil's Breath
Horizontal Hold
The Face Out Front
Freeze Frame
Jump Cut

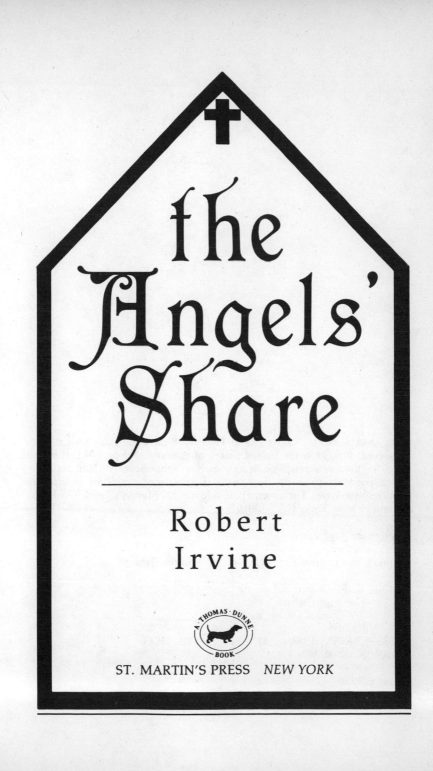

the Angels' Share

Robert
Irvine

A THOMAS DUNNE BOOK

ST. MARTIN'S PRESS   NEW YORK

Design by Jaye Zimet

Library of Congress Cataloging-in-Publication Data

Irvine, R. R. (Robert R.)
     The angels' share.
     "A Thomas Dunne book."
     I. Title.
PS3559.R65A85 1989   813'.54   88–35941
ISBN 0–312–02862–8

First Edition

10   9   8   7   6   5   4   3   2   1

To Robert Campbell

1

Standing on the scorching sidewalk across the street from the temple, Moroni Traveler focused on Salt Lake City's ten thousand–foot eastern barrier known as the Wasatch Front. The mountains, still tipped with snow in July, stored enough water each winter to keep the rivers running all year around, enough to irrigate a desert and create Brigham Young's land of Zion.

At the moment the 10 A.M. sidewalk temperature in the promised land was one hundred degrees.

Traveler shuffled his feet to avoid blisters and waved at Mad Bill, who was picketing the Mormon temple. Known as the Sandwich Prophet, Bill carried his usual sandwich board. Today's said: GOD IS MAKING ZION HOT AS HELL.

As soon as Bill acknowledged the wave, Traveler dashed inside the Chester Building. Vaulted ceilings and marble floors made the lobby feel air conditioned, an illusion that would be dispelled when afternoon sun hit the front windows. The building's owner, Barney Chester, was sampling the wares of his old-fashioned cigar stand. He blew smoke and words at Traveler. "You have clients waiting upstairs."

According to the Regulator Clock on the wall, Traveler's ten-fifteen appointment was early. He shrugged at Barney and headed for the elevator. Its operator, Nephi Bates, saw him coming and turned up the volume on a small cassette player that hung from a strap around his neck. The Mormon Tabernacle Choir sang out:

> "Israel, Israel, God is calling—
> calling from the lands of woe;
> Babylon the Great is falling;
> God shall all her towers o'erthrow.
> Come to Zion."

The third and top floor of the Chester Building was a good ten degrees hotter than the lobby, but still cooler than the streets outside. Father and daughter, or so Traveler assumed, were waiting in the hall outside his door.

"I'm Newell Farnsworth. This is my daughter, Suzanne," the man confirmed. "I called yesterday for an appointment."

"Sorry I kept you waiting."

"We're early."

The daughter sighed as if to say punctuality was her own personal, parentally imposed burden.

Traveler unlocked the door and ushered them inside. His was a corner office with two windows, one facing north toward the temple, the other looking out on Main Street to the east. At the moment the Main Street window was acting as a magnifying glass. As a result the room felt on the verge of spontaneous combustion.

Traveler's tan polyester slacks and white knit sports shirt clung like a wet suit as he opened both windows, hoping for the cross-ventilation Barney had promised when first showing him the office six months ago. What came in was a hot west wind, carrying with it the rotten-egg smell of the Great Salt Lake. From the streets below rose the sound of wind-whipped flags, part of the Pioneer Day decorations, which were flapping as noisily as banners at a used-car lot. The celebration was still four days away, July 24, the anniversary of the date in 1847 when the first Latter-day Saints—LDS, as they called themselves—arrived in

Salt Lake. They'd crossed half a continent, including the Rocky Mountains, to blaze the Mormon Trail. Traveler's great-grandmother had been with them. But family zeal ran out long before he was born.

"We have our choice," he said. "What passes for fresh air or heatstroke."

"The lake doesn't bother me," Farnsworth said as though he enjoyed the smell.

His daughter sighed again.

"The building's owner doesn't believe in air conditioning. He says it would be sacrilege to tamper with a landmark." Traveler winked at his namesake, the Angel Moroni perched atop a temple spire across the street. The figure's gold plate was all that kept it from tarnishing like everything else.

"Moroni Traveler is a good Mormon name," Farnsworth said, his voice slightly off-key, probably with embarrassment, something that often happened when people came to see a private detective. He and his daughter settled into the two clients' chairs that faced the desk. Traveler sat behind the desk, folded his hands, and studied the pair closely.

Farnsworth was gray at the temples and looked to be about forty, wearing sharply creased gray slacks and a short-sleeved dress shirt with a tie. He had heavily muscled forearms, blunt hands, and a worry-free face that reminded Traveler of every Mormon bishop he'd ever met.

His daughter was small-boned and overweight, on the verge of escaping her teens and maybe even the blemishes on her chin. A pale-green tent dress failed to camouflage her excesses.

"You look like a weight-lifter to me," Farnsworth said, still avoiding the subject of the visit.

"I was when I played football. Now I prefer to use my head."

"I followed your career. A Utah boy in professional football isn't all that common."

"On the phone," Traveler prompted, "you said something about a missing person."

"Your firm was recommended by a colleague of mine. Another dentist. I take it there are two of you."

Despite the lettering on the door, MORONI TRAVELER & SON, Traveler's father insisted on calling himself Martin, since he hated being named for an angel.

"Who's missing?" Traveler asked.

"My daughter's fiancé."

Traveler nodded encouragement.

"Suzanne has been out of high school for two years now," Farnsworth went on.

That made her twenty, Traveler thought, slightly older than his original assessment.

"She's been attending Westminster College, studying business while waiting for her fiancé to get back from his mission."

Susanne blinked, causing Traveler to notice her reddened eyes. After a moment she wet her pale lips as if intending to speak.

Her father beat her to it. " 'The ax is laid at the root of the trees and every tree that bringeth not forth good fruit shall be hewn down and cast into the fire.' "

Suzanne surprised Traveler with a smile. "Daddy likes to give people the impression that he's a religious scholar. But he only memorizes those passages in *The Book of Mormon* that suit his purposes. He thinks I should be having babies by now."

"I'm a bishop in the church, Mr. Traveler, though I may be stepping down soon because of the growth of my dental practice. The more patients who depend on me, the less time I have to devote to scriptures."

Suzanne's left eye, the one that her father couldn't see, winked. "Daddy was asked to step down. The church likes to maximize its tithe. The more money he makes, the more they get from him."

"You see what this young man has done to us,"

Farnsworth complained, though his tone was more amused than condemning. "His absence has set her against me."

"My father wants me married. So do I."

"I still don't know the name of the man we're after," Traveler said.

"What am I thinking of?" Farnsworth tapped himself on the forehead. "His name is Heber Armstrong."

Now there was a good Mormon name, most likely derived from Herber J. Grant, a former president and prophet of the church. One of Traveler's classmates at Roosevelt Junior High had been named Heber. Everyone called him Heeb, a nickname he had detested to the point of fist fights.

Suzane took a photograph from her green plastic purse and slid it across the desk.

"That was taken about two years ago, just before Heber left on his mission."

The young man in the photo was gangly. But then Suzanne had been that way too when the picture was taken, fifty pounds ago. He had light hair and was squinting into both sun and camera lens.

She held out her left hand to display the small diamond ring that was half buried in the flesh of her finger. "It was the day we got engaged. Right after that he was called on a mission to England. He disappeared a month or so before he was due to come home."

"What do the police here say?"

"That England is out of their jurisdiction," Farnsworth answered. "That it's more properly a church matter."

"And the English authorities?"

"As a bishop I know a lot of important people there, in and out of the church. For months they've been telling me that everything possible was being done to find him. But nothing happened until the day before yesterday."

Farnsworth stopped speaking and looked to his daughter.

"That's when I saw Heber," she said. "He's here, back in Salt Lake, and hasn't even called me. That's why I know something terrible has happened." She rubbed her eyes, making them redder than ever.

"Suzy was on the bus at the time. By the time she got off at the next stop and went back he'd disappeared into the ZCMI."

Traveler could see the upper facade of the Zion's Cooperative Mercantile Institution from his eastern window. In pioneer times, the ZCMI had been Brigham Young's attempt to keep the faithful from spending their money with gentile merchants, gentile being the LDS term for all non-Mormons.

Farnsworth laid one of his blunt dentist's hands on his daughter's shoulder. "Maybe it was just wishful thinking on your part, honey."

She closed her eyes. Continued movement beneath her lids suggested that she was watching some inner drama unfold. With a sigh she cradled her stomach as a pregnant woman might do. "Herber needs me. I can feel it inside."

"Are you certain it was your fiancé?" Traveler asked.

"He looked right at me. I'm sure he saw me. His eyes frightened me though. They were desperate."

"How long does it usually take to find someone who's missing?" Farnsworth asked.

"That depends on whether they want to be found or not. If this young man is in town, I ought to be able to come up with something in a reasonable time. But you have to be prepared for bad news, Miss Farnsworth. He could be avoiding you because he no longer wants to get married."

"I understand," she said, though everything about her, her expression, her tone, said otherwise.

Her father cleared his throat. "Do you have a dental plan, Mr. Traveler?"

"I don't trade services, if that's what you're suggesting. My fee is two hundred and fifty dollars a day, plus expenses."

Farnsworth fingered his front teeth as if taking comfort

from what he knew best. "Suzy hasn't gone out with a man in two years now. I want grandchildren before I'm too old to enjoy them. So do whatever you have to."

"A week in advance is my usual retainer. Whatever I don't use will be refunded."

Farnsworth snapped his teeth in shock, but wrote out a check just the same.

"I'll need more information," Traveler said as soon as he'd exchanged the check for a receipt. "Did you think to contact Customs to see if Armstrong has reentered the country?"

"The church reported that he had. It also said there's no reason to believe that he's returned to Zion."

"What about letters, Miss Farnsworth? When was the last time you heard from your fiancé?"

"About four months ago, I think. I wrote twice a week right from the beginning, when he was still a greenie."

Traveler smiled. He hadn't heard that expression in a long time. It referred to missionaries who were just beginning their tour of duty.

"How often did he write back?"

"They kept him awfully busy. I understood that. He wrote whenever he could."

"Did he ever indicate to you that anything might be wrong?"

"No." Her head shook vigorously enough to keep her eyes from meeting his. She continued to avoid his stare even after the shaking stopped.

Traveler swiveled his desk chair and stared out at the temple, where the Angel Moroni shimmered in heat waves thick enough to make his trumpet wobble. He felt certain that she was holding back information, something that couldn't be said in front of her father.

He went full circle until he was facing his clients again. "What about Heber's family? Have they heard from him?"

"I spoke with them this morning before coming here,"

Farnsworth answered. "They claim they haven't been in touch with him."

"Do you have any reason to doubt that?"

Both father and daughter shook their heads.

"I'll probably talk to them anyway."

Suzanne provided an address high enough on the Avenues to be somewhere near the LDS hospital.

Her father said, "We used to live down the block from them. But that was before we moved to The Cove." At the mention of The Cove his tone changed; it let Traveler know that only professional men like dentists could afford to live in that exclusive enclave at the base of the Wasatch Mountains. Traveler had hiked that area as a boy, when deer still roamed freely and beaver dams marked every stream.

"I'll need the names of his close friends."

"Most of them were at seminary with him," Suzanne said. An LDS seminary stood across the street from just about every high school in Utah, creating the illusion of separation of church and state.

"There was Ned Cody, Kent Brown, and John Neff. They also played basketball together in the church league."

Traveler wrote the names down on a notepad. "Do you know their addresses?"

"Not specifically, but they lived somewhere in the neighborhood. You ought to be able to find their parents in the phone book."

Traveler pretended to study his notes. "Were there other women?"

Out of the corner of his eye he saw her wince. "The only thing I know for sure is that when I'm nervous and alone, I eat too much."

"God is with you, honey, and so is your daddy," her father said softly.

"Over the last two years I've gained so much weight Heber won't want me anymore."

"I'd like to talk to your daughter privately," Traveler said.

"Suzy and I have no secrets."

The girl took hold of her father's hand. "It might be best, Daddy. Sometimes it's easier talking to strangers."

Farnsworth glared at Traveler. "I'll be right outside in the hall."

The girl began to cry softly as soon as the door closed. Traveler took a small pack of tissues from his desk and handed it to her.

He didn't speak until she blew her nose. "I can't help unless you tell me the truth."

She took a deep breath. "When Heber left for England I told him, 'Don't worry. You'll never get a Dear John letter from me.'"

"And was he just as faithful?"

Her eyes closed; her chin dropped onto her chest. "He mentioned a woman in one of his letters. Nothing about love, only that he'd converted her to the church."

"That seems normal enough."

"Her name was Alma. She was the only convert he ever wrote about by name."

"Is there anything else you haven't told me?"

Tears kept her from answering for a few moments. In the silence he could hear her father pacing the marble hallway outside.

"In his last letter he told me not to wait for him, that he wasn't coming back. He said he'd lost his faith and called himself a missionary of the damned."

2

Before leaving the office, Traveler left a note for his father, to which he paper-clipped Newell Farnsworth's check.

Martin: We have a client at last. His bishop's face tells me that you might be wise to cash his check immediately. I'll tell you about our missing missionary at dinner.

When he reached the lobby, Barney was behind his cigar counter dispensing coffee to Mad Bill and Charlie Redwine. The three of them raised their cups at Traveler's approach.

"Bill says God had turned his back on Zion," Barney reported.

"And Charlie?" Traveler said.

"He doesn't care," Bill said, speaking for his Indian companion as usual. "He says the Navajos have been living in hell ever since the white man arrived." He pointed at the nearest of the lobby's Doric columns and then raised his finger, as if following the path of the marble to the vaulted ceiling overhead. There Brigham Young led a wagon train across the length of a depression-era fresco. "Religion in the hands of a white man is a dangerous thing, Charlie says. God is—"

"Moroni," Barney interrupted, "would you care to flaunt the Word of Wisdom and join us in a cup of coffee?" He never joked about church commandments in the presence of those who might be offended.

"It's too hot," Traveler said.

Barney handed him a paper cup anyway. It smelled of wine.

"Charlie spiked it," Bill explained as he disbursed sticks of spearmint gum, the usual remedy against the smell of sin in Mormon country.

Today Bill was wearing khaki shorts and a T-shirt that said PRAY FOR SALVATION on the front. Usually he wore long robes to go along with sandwich boards. He was Traveler's height and thin everywhere except his stomach.

Bill gulped his coffee and said, "Sodom and Gomorrah is at hand. When that happens I'll take my rightful place as true prophet."

Traveler only grunted. He'd heard it all before.

"Don't look so skeptical, Moroni. This time it's true. Even Charlie agrees."

Everyone looked at the Navajo, whose expression might just as well have been carved on a cigar store Indian.

Bill said, "Lead the way, Charlie."

The Indian hitched his Levi's and headed for the revolving door, an art deco relic from the thirties. Traveler followed in his aromatic wake, a mixture of alcohol, tobacco, sweat, and hair oil. Barney and Bill brought up the rear.

The Navajo stopped in front of a newspaper rack that was chained to a lamp post at the corner. Behind the Plexiglass cover a huge black headline declared: WOMAN BUTCHERED.

As Traveler stared at it, heat from the sidewalk came right through the soles of his shoes. Charlie, who was wearing moccasins, began shifting his weight from foot to foot and humming as if he were performing some kind of ritual dance.

Traveler leaned over to read the small print but it was hidden beneath the fold.

Charlie held his hand out like the experienced panhandler he was. Traveler filled his palm with loose change. The Indian nodded and pounded the rack with his fist until it sprang open, providing him with a free copy of the *Tribune*'s street edition.

As soon as Traveler accepted the newspaper, Charlie pocketed the coins and then danced down the block toward West Temple Street, quickly disappearing around the corner.

"Godspeed," Bill murmured before standing on tiptoe to read over Traveler's shoulder while Barney, a foot shorter, began pounding on the newspaper rack in hopes of freeing his own copy.

Despite the size of the headline, the story was only four single-sentence paragraphs.

A savage killer struck early this morning, brutally stabbing a young woman to death in Glendale Park on the west side of town.

Police say the partially clad woman, as yet unidentified, may have been the victim of some kind of ritual mutilation.

Tests are still being conducted to determine if the murdered woman was sexually molested.

Officer Tim Marshall, who discovered the body when responding to an anonymous phone call, told the *Tribune*, "I've never seen anything like it. And I hope I never do again."

"You see," Bill said, "God has turned his back on Zion."

Traveler, whose feet felt as if they were on the verge of broiling, only shook his head. Arguing with Bill never got him anywhere.

"My turn will come." Bill laid a hand across Traveler's

shoulder. "The Sandwich Prophet ruling in Zion with my own version of the Angel Moroni at my side."

With his other hand, Bill gestured to Barney, who reluctantly allowed himself to be taken under the prophet's wing.

"My faithful flock," Bill said.

Traveler ducked free. "Someone's chasing your first apostle."

Despite the heat, Charlie was loping toward them up South Temple.

"They're gaining." Barney pointed at the two young men in suits and ties who were close on the Indian's heels.

"I recognize them," Bill said. "They and their kind prey on Lamanites."

Traveler raised his eyebrows at Barney. They both knew that *The Book of Mormon* referred to Indians like Charlie as Lamanites, declaring them to be direct descendants of the lost tribe of Israel. Jesus was said to have honored the Lamanites by journeying among them as the great white God Quetzalcoatl.

"Come on," Bill said, trotting forward. "We've got to save him."

Timing was such that they all met in front of the Chester Building, even the two pursuers, who were totally out of breath and sweating so badly their gray suit coats were soaked through around the armpits. In this kind of desert heat such dress marked them as either FBI agents or Mormon missionaries, both of whom traveled in pairs, adhering to strict codes.

Looking at these two, Traveler decided they were too young to be anything but agents of faith.

Charlie whispered something in Bill's ear.

"They picked Charlie up going into the Era Antique Shop," Bill relayed.

Charlie confided something else.

"They interrupted his pilgrimage before he could provide an offering for our church."

Traveler resisted the temptation to translate that, since the look on Barney's face said he already understood. Charlie thought the white man owed him a living, so he helped himself by shoplifting wherever the pickings were easiest.

"Local missionaries are the worst," Bill rambled on. "Since they never leave Utah, their targets are more limited. Seeing Charlie must have been like manna from heaven."

"He didn't have enough time to whisper all that in your ear," Barney complained.

"We have our own language."

The two missionaries were staring at Bill's T-shirt.

"We know you," one of them said.

"They think I'm the devil," Bill said, looking pleased.

"I'm looking for a missionary who's here in Salt Lake," Traveler told them. "Maybe you know him. His name is Heber Armstrong."

The pair stepped back almost in unison. The look in their eyes said it was Traveler who was the devil, not Bill.

3

The address Suzanne Farnsworth had given Traveler lay high on the city's north bench, on 8th Avenue between F and G streets. To get there Traveler drove toward the Wasatch Mountains, whose glaciered peaks reminded him of the crusted jaw of some ancient carnivore. Brigham Young, fleeing from religious persecution in Illinois, had crossed those heights at the head of a pioneer wagon train in 1847. For years afterward the Wasatch served as a barricade against his eastern enemies, better than any manmade citadel. On the west lay another another vast barrier, the Great Salt Lake. Between the two of them, he built his city. His glory, the faithful called it, a town laid out according to holy logic, with all life radiating out from its hub, the temple. Even the street names were part of his religious master plan. Those directly adjacent to the temple were named East Temple, North Temple, West Temple, and South Temple. Next came First East, First West, First South, and First North. Farther out were lettered streets and avenues, a rational progression all the way to the city limits. Recent years had brought with them the secular chaos of progress, until now Brigham's city was called Greater Salt Lake, with over a million people and everything that went with them.

By the time Traveler found the number he was looking

for, a red warning light glared from the Ford's dashboard. The car was overheated and so was he. When he stepped out onto the street the asphalt felt gummy underfoot. He estimated the temperature at a hundred and five.

The house was one of those bleak two-story brick bungalows so common to the Avenues, built to survive winters instead of scrutiny. Erected on rising ground, it had small windows, a gray tar-paper roof, and a rickety wooden stairway clinging to one outside wall. Some time in the distant past it had been converted to a duplex.

A wooden porch in need of paint, with a waist-high railing, ran across the front of the house. The porch roof, supported by white columns that looked vaguely Ionic, provided a balcony for the second floor. At the moment, the house was closed against the heat, with shades drawn at every window.

The backyard, part of which Traveler could see down a long grease-spotted driveway, was dominated by a magnificent elm tree. At the point where its lowest limbs branched out from the trunk, a good-sized tree house had been built. Though dilapidated by time and tilted by tree growth, the structure still looked impressive. It had a pointed, church-like roof, complete with a wooden cross at its apex. Its one window, opaque with grime, was long and narrow, as was the door, still in place despite being out of plumb.

As a boy Traveler had longed for such a hideout. He was mulling over the trees of his youth, comparing them with the elm, as he mounted the steps to the front porch. He failed to notice the man in the wicker chair until he stood up.

Traveler tensed. "Is this the Armstrong house?"

The man looked Samoan, or maybe Tongan. Both countries were prime target areas for Mormon missionaries. Both produced big, tough men, like the one facing him. Whether missionaries recruited them out of religious zeal or to fill the ranks of Brigham Young University's football team Traveler didn't know. This one ignored the question.

"BYU?" Traveler guessed out loud.

The man, who was the right age to play football, nodded. He had a fifty-pound edge on Traveler, who himself weighed close to two twenty.

"Samoan?" Traveler said.

The nod gave way to a negative headshake.

The last Tongan that Traveler had played against in professional ball bit when the referees weren't looking.

"You look like a tackle," Traveler said.

"Nose guard."

"And here?"

"I keep my eye on things."

"By that I take it you mean the Armstrongs."

The Tongan folded his arms, quite an achievement considering how much muscle got in the way.

"Are they home?"

"Go ahead and knock. I won't stop you."

The door opened before Traveler had time to raise his hand. The woman who stood there, squinting at him against the sunlight, was using both hands to tuck strands of gray hair beneath a wig of shiny red curls that bounced with a life of their own.

"Mrs. Armstrong?" he asked, reading her as grandmother instead of mother.

"That's right.

"I'm looking for Heber Armstrong."

The porch creaked as the Tongan shifted his weight.

"His fiancé has asked me to help find him," Traveler added.

A man appeared at Mrs. Armstrong's shoulder. He glared at Traveler. "Just who the heck are you?"

Traveler removed his wallet and displayed a photostat of his license.

"Heber's our son all right," the man admitted.

Traveler had been expecting a couple in their forties, maybe even late thirties. After all, Mormons married young, so it wasn't uncommon for missionaries to have parents still bearing offspring. But the Armstrongs were well beyond that age. Sixty, he estimated, with the same kind of worn-out, depression faces that haunted the farms of southern Utah.

"I've never seen a private detective before," the man said. "Except on TV." He had the look of someone who'd recently lost weight. His T-shirt, stained around the armpits, was too big for him. So were his work pants. His slippers were mashed down around the heels.

He held out a leathery hand. "I'm Klaus Armstrong. You might as well come in. Isn't that right, Doris?"

His wife answered with a glare hostile enough to make the Tongan flex his muscles.

"The longer we stand here," Klaus said, "the more heat we let inside."

"We don't have to talk to him." Mrs. Armstrong adjusted her wig with a jerk hard enough to start its Shirley Temple curls vibrating again.

"Come on, Mother. I feel sorry for that Farnsworth girl."

"You feel sorry for everyone but me," she said, but moved out of the way so Traveler could step across the threshold. As he did so, the Tongan went back to his porch chair.

Klaus led the way into a small, darkened living room. "We don't like turning on the lights in this kind of weather. It'll be a scorcher in here soon enough."

As soon as Traveler found his way to an overstuffed chair, he closed his eyes to help them adjust to the gloom. He didn't open them again until Klaus said, "I never thought to see a private eye here in Zion."

The Armstrongs had arranged themselves side by side on a sofa facing him. Flanking the sofa were end tables crammed with photographs in stand-up frames. Every available surface in the room—the TV, the mantel, the bookcase—were similarly arrayed. He assumed all of the photos to be pictures of Heber, though the childhood poses bore little resemblance to the young man in Suzanne Farnsworth's snapshot.

"Tell me what's being done to find your missing son," he said.

Klaus started to speak but Doris silenced him with a jab of her elbow. "Suzanne phoned here yesterday. She didn't have the courtesy to come in person. No, indeed. Nobody in that family has set foot in this neighborhood since they moved to The Cove. They're too good for the likes of us now."

"Now, Mother," her husband chided.

She gave him a scathing look. "I'll tell this detective the same thing I did her. If our son had come home, don't you think we'd know it?"

"That wasn't my question."

"You'd think our son had committed a crime or something. But I'm his mother and I know better. He's a victim, not a criminal. You can be sure of that."

"I was told that he disappeared while on a mission. Is that correct?"

She pulled a tissue from the neck of her faded house-dress and dabbed her nose. "As soon as he went missing, they told us to prepare for the worst. I won't do that. Not ever. My boy will come home to me. A mother knows such things."

She lowered her head, allowing her husband to speak. "Everybody—the police, the church—said the same thing. When someone disappears you've got to figure the worst. We'd go to England and look for him ourselves but we don't have the money, not after paying Heber's expenses."

That, Traveler knew, was the Mormon way, parents and friends paying for a missionary's work so the church itself would never be out of pocket.

"Suzanne Farnsworth is certain that she saw your son here in town two days ago."

"Hot flashes, if you ask me," Doris said.

"Now, Mother," her husband said, taking hold of her

arm. "Be charitable. It's probably just wishful thinking on Suzanne's part. We can't blame her for that."

The woman broke free of his grasp to wander around the room, fondling one framed photograph after another. She kissed the one that showed her son in a Little League uniform.

"Heber was a late-life child," Klaus explained. "We'd just about given up having children when he came along."

His wife clasped the frame against her bosom. "We never stopped praying then and I won't stop now." She sank down on her knees. "We named him after one of our beloved prophets in the hope that the church would be his true calling."

"Don't get the wrong idea," Klaus said. "He was a regular kid. He played baseball all the way through high school."

His wife nodded. "That was part of God's plan. When our Heber got to England he organized a team to attract young people. It was a wonderful success. He set a record for conversions in a single day. I have a letter from his mission leader that says so."

Klaus's fingers intertwined as if preparing for prayer. "His third baseman was the first to join the church. Soon after, the whole team did. Heber had no way of knowing that one of their parents would attack him."

"He was fighting the Lord's battle," Doris added.

"He had no choice. He had to defend himself."

Until that moment Traveler had never considered the fact that each convert left behind family, friends, and clergymen, any one of whom might decide to retaliate against Mormonism. It was as good a motive as any for Heber's disappearance.

"He broke the man's nose," Klaus added with a sense of pride. "There was threat of a lawsuit but nothing came of it."

"Did your son have any close friends here in the neighborhood?" Traveler asked.

Husband and wife exchanged questioning glances. It was Klaus who said, "They're all away on missions except one."

"Who's that?"

"Ned Cody, but he's lost his way from the church."

"He works at the Dairy Queen on Eleventh East," Doris said, as if that were hell itself.

"And the Tongan outside?" Traveler asked.

Cartilage popped in her knees as she struggled to her feet. "He's a friend of our bishop who needed a place to stay for the summer. We're letting him live in the apartment upstairs."

"In this kind of weather," her husband went on, "the heat up there is unbearable. That's why he spends most of his time on the front porch. Even that gets too hot in late afternoon when there's no more shade."

"He looks like a bodyguard to me," Traveler said.

Mrs. Armstrong turned away, pretending to dust her photograph.

"Or a jailer," Traveler added.

Klaus, though appearing to stare Traveler in the face, focused somewhere else in time.

"Did your son live here at home before he left on his mission?"

The woman spun around. "He didn't live with that girl, if that's what you're asking."

"I was just wondering about his room, that's all. I thought maybe I could see it."

"Why?"

"If I'm going to look for him, I'd like to know him a little better."

"Know him," she echoed. "How can you know him?" Her voice caught.

Klaus came to her aid. "It can't do any harm, Mother. You stay here. I'll show Mr. Traveler around."

Heber's room was small, no more than ten by ten. Yet into it had been squeezed a double bed, a dresser, two chairs, and a large bookcase that held three small TV sets, plus half a dozen textbooks on television journalism and videotape editing.

"My boy was majoring in communications at BYU before the call came for his mission. Television fascinated him, even as a youngster. I can't tell you how many times he asked me to add a room onto the house so he could have his own TV studio. Every time he did, I told him the same thing. We can't afford it." His eyes glistened with moisture. "I'm sorry now that I retired from the post office early. I should have taken out a mortgage, anything." The last word came out as a sob.

Traveler looked around the room to give the man time to compose himself. There were no photographs, only a world map on the wall with a red pin marking London, England.

"Heber was our whole life. He still is."

Traveler thanked him and left the house, pausing on the sidewalk to look back at the Tongan who, in turn, stared at the detective. There was a time, Traveler thought, when he could have taken a nose guard that size. He'd weighed twenty pounds more in those days, without giving away any of the speed a linebacker needed.

He was about to get in his car when Klaus Armstrong came out of the house and down the stairs.

"I wanted to show you something," he said, pointing toward the elm in the backyard. "Heber built that tree house himself, without any help from me. He drew up the plans himself."

Traveler shaded his eyes to study the tree house. As he did so, he caught a glimpse of something metallic circling the trunk, probably the anchor for an old-fashioned clothesline.

"He was ten years old at the time. As an act of faith, he said he wanted to build his own personal church."

The man shook his head at the memory. "Thinking back on it now, I wonder if it wasn't sacrilege to say something like that."

4

The Dairy Queen was once Traveler's favorite stop after playing American Legion ball at Municipal Park. Looking at the place now, he wondered how teenagers ever managed to survive their appetites.

At the moment a dozen people were lined up at the two service windows, ordering soft ice-cream cones and milkshakes to beat the heat. Traveler joined the longest line, the one leading to a young man who looked the right age to be Ned Cody. Whoever he was, he was moving in slow motion compared to his female counterpart at the next window.

When Traveler's turn came he ordered a large cone and paid for it with a ten-dollar bill. "If you're Ned Cody, the change is yours for a few minutes of your time."

"I'm Cody," he said. A spark of enthusiasm flared in his dull eyes. "Who the hell are you?"

"Someone who's looking for a friend of yours."

"Do I look like the kind of guy who'd sell out a friend?"

"Would you like it better if I called him an acquaintance?"

"You're holding up the line," Cody said.

"You can keep the money. I'll wait until you can take a break before introducing myself properly."

"Suit yourself."

A quarter of an hour passed, with Traveler doing his best to stay in a narrow strip of shade cast by the Dairy Queen's overhanging roof, before business slacked off. The moment that happened Cody eased out a side door, leaned against the wall, and lit a cigarette while waiting for Traveler to join him. Up close, he had eyes that said he smoked more than tobacco.

The loose sleeves of his sweat-stained T-shirt had been rolled high enough to expose armpit hair and a skull-and-bones tattoo over his vaccination scar. His arms were stick-thin. He had a narrow face, with skin so taut that his skull showed through, and lips that failed to cover his teeth. As a result, he reminded Traveler of an animal that would bite if you got too close.

"The church says your body is a temple," Traveler told him. "Defacing it is a sin."

"Eight-fifty doesn't buy much time."

Traveler handed him another ten. The sight of it brought a greedy smile to Cody's inadequate lips. He'd come a long way from seminary and the church basketball league.

"I still don't know your name, mister."

Traveler took out his wallet and flipped it open to his investigator's license. Judging by the way Cody squinted at it, he couldn't focus his eyes properly.

"So what do you want from me?"

"Heber Armstrong."

"Shit. What are you after him for, praying without a license?"

"He's missing."

Cody drew on his cigarette and blew smoke in Traveler's face. "It couldn't have happened to a nicer guy."

"Why do you say that?"

"Don't get me wrong. Heeb was okay at first. But once they got their hands on him in seminary he went kind of crazy. Turned him into a regular fanatic. Everything he did after that had to be part of God's plan. It didn't matter if he

was working for the church, playing ball, or talking about
that TV studio of his, everything was God's will to Heeb.
'Do or die for Jesus,' that's what he used to say. Christ, it
was enough to make you sick."

"What TV studio are you talking about?"

"I never saw it myself. But it was all Heeb talked about
there for a while. He was like that. He'd get on a subject
and beat it to death."

"Do you know where it was?"

"Look, mister. He had this idea of making religious
movies for the church, or some damn thing. I wasn't interested, period. I was already getting more preaching than I
could stand at home from my old man. For all I know, that
studio was just another of Heeb's pipe dreams."

"I'd like to hear about those dreams of his."

Cody's puny shoulders rose and fell in a shrug that
seemed to deny all responsibility for his spoken word.
"You know the kind of thing I mean. Big talk that was
nothing but bullshit. Like the time he told me we were
going to win the church league's basketball championship."

"And did you?"

"Are you kidding? We weren't good enough to be second-rate."

As far as Traveler could see, second-rate was too high a
ranking for the likes of Cody.

"Describe Heber for me," Traveler said. "Tell me what
kind of person he was."

Cody's shoulders twitched, another disclaimer.

Reluctantly, Traveler plucked a new bill from his wallet.

"He couldn't make a jump-shot if his life depended on
it," Cody said quickly, his eyes never leaving the money.

"That's not what I meant." Traveler kept a firm grasp
on the note. "What was he like in seminary, for instance?"

Cody didn't answer until the money changed hands and
was tucked safely into his jeans. "Who the hell listened? I

only went because my old man made me. I could have used a study period in school instead of sermons."

"Have you heard from Heber recently?"

"No way. I stay away from do-gooders."

"What about girlfriends?"

"Like I said, Heeb was a do-gooder. He had one girl all through high school. Her name was Suzy something-or-other. If you ask me, he never even plowed her furrow."

"Do you have any idea who Heber might contact if he came back to town unexpectedly? Close friends, for instance?"

"I stopped going to church a long time ago."

The Dairy Queen's side door opened. A young girl, Cody's co-worker, poked her head out long enough to say, "We're getting busy again, Ned. I need help."

Cody flipped away his cigarette and started to follow her.

"One more question," Traveler said. "When was the last time you saw him?"

"That's easy. The day he caught me smoking and said I was going to hell."

5

From the Dairy Queen, Traveler drove directly to the new LDS office building at South Temple and Main, the city's preeminent intersection where a bronze Brigham Young stood forever with his back to the temple.

Until recently the office building had been the Hotel Utah, perhaps the finest in the West. Now ten stories of white terra-cotta brick were filled with men like Willis Tanner, a troubleshooter for the church who had been Traveler's best friend in junior high school. Before religion got in the way.

Closed-circuit television cameras and youthful guards with zealots' eyes monitored Traveler's entrance. He wondered where they kept their Uzis.

Security was a Mormon passion, and paranoia. It went all the way back to Brigham Young, whose great obsession was to preserve Utah for his, the chosen, people. To do that, he preached isolation from gentiles. He set up a spy system to keep track of wayward laity who traded with gentile merchants. At one point he went so far as to order the all-seeing eye placed over the doorway of every Mormon shop. That way, the faithful would know when they were sinning. Too many such sins and they could expect a visit from Brigham's avenging angels, known as Danites, among other things.

At the information desk Traveler gave his name and intention to a young man who looked a year or two beyond mission age, say twenty-two. Instead of telephoning Tanner's office, the receptionist typed Traveler's name into a computer terminal, pushed a button, and then sat back, his gaze alternating between the detective and the amber screen.

"I remember when people used to send messages like that in pneumatic tubes," Traveler said.

The young man smiled grimly, the kind of look reserved for young children and the senile. His terminal beeped.

"I'm sorry. Mr. Tanner isn't available at the moment. I suggest you make an appointment."

"With you?"

"You'll have to call."

"What number?" Traveler asked, knowing he already had it back at the office.

"I can't give that out."

Since Brigham's day the Danites of security had been replaced by retired FBI agents, so Traveler knew better than to argue.

"Tell Willis I'll be in my office," he said. "Tell him it's important."

"We've got church work," Traveler announced as soon as he saw his father standing at the window, slump-shouldered and staring out at the temple.

But Martin didn't provoke as expected. For that matter he didn't say a word, didn't even turn around.

"It was a joke. We're working for a missionary's girlfriend."

"Fine."

"It's better than nothing."

"Uh-huh."

"It might even be interesting. When I spoke to the missionary's parents, I got the impression that something funny was going on. Either that or I'm losing my touch."

Martin sighed and turned around. His face, drawn and pale, looked ten years older than it had this morning.

"Jesus, Dad, What's wrong?"

"Who said anything was wrong?"

"You look exhausted."

"What do you expect from a man my age, tap-dancing?"

Traveler stared his father in the face. Martin's answering look of innocence lacked conviction. Traveler changed the subject. "Did you get a chance to cash the check?"

"In this damned heat? You've been taken in like everybody else, believing those stories about old people being able to handle the heat better. Move to the desert, they say. Someplace like Palm Springs. It's good for your joints and your arthritis. Well, I'm here to tell you it's all bullshit. The only thing you ever see in places like that is old farts more dead than alive. And a few lizards."

"Say no more. You took your physical exam today, didn't you? You're down on doctors for the next twenty-four hours."

In the instant before Martin turned away, Traveler's saw something he didn't understand in his father's eyes.

Traveler dropped an arm over his father's shoulder. "It's no big deal if Doc Murphy wants you to sit out in the sun somewhere and take it easy."

"Like all quacks, he wants to take more tests. And spend more of my money. I'm supposed to go back in the morning, if you can believe it."

Dr. Murphy had been treating them both for years. In all that time he'd never asked for such a return visit.

"Is there something you're not telling me, Dad?"

Before Martin could answer, the door opened and in walked Willis Tanner with a Tongan in tow. This one made the nose guard at the Armstrong house look stunted.

"I got your message, Moroni. So here I am, ready and willing to talk. Alone, though."

"Like the sign says on the door," Martin said, settling

into the chair behind his son's desk, "Moroni Traveler and Son. State your business."

Tanner held out his hands in a pleading gesture. "How long have we known each other, Mo? Twenty-five years, isn't it? A quarter century, for heaven's sake."

Traveler dragged one of the two clients' chairs around the side of the desk and sat down next to Martin.

His father coughed. "The first time I laid eyes on you, Willis, you were smoking behind the house. Do you remember that?"

Tanner ran a hand over the bristles of his crewcut, a style he'd retained since junior high. "I seem to remember that I was trying to save your son from sin."

"I caught you doing something else too. Or have you forgotten that?"

"You win. As long as what I have to say stays in the family, you're welcome to listen in, Martin."

"And your bodyguard?" Traveler asked, nodding at the Tongan.

"Buddy is my alter-ego this summer."

Traveler willed himself not to blink as he stared at Tanner. "He makes two Tongans in one day. Would you call that coincidence?"

As usual, his friend squinted when under stress. It was a habit he'd acquired as a teenager, along with astigmatism. "Buddy would have been on the varsity squad at BYU this fall if he hadn't been red-shirted."

Tanner removed his glasses to massage his eyelids. "In the meantime, he's earning room and board doing odd jobs for the church."

"What position does he play?"

"That hasn't been decided yet."

"Why is it, Willis, I have the feeling we're not talking about football?"

Tanner smiled and slipped his rimless glasses back into place. His squint was gone for the moment. "Mo, you never change."

"Neither do you," Martin said. "I should have blistered your backside when I had the chance."

Tanner sat in the remaining chair, widened his smile and folded his hands. "Here I am, doubly blessed by being in the same room with two Moronis."

"The name is Martin. It has been ever since I won my first fight in school. That was a long time ago, but I can still take you, old man or not."

The Tongan snorted through his flat nose.

"It's all right, Buddy. You can wait outside."

Martin pointed a finger at Tanner. "I don't care how important you are. I don't trust you."

Tanner waved Buddy on his way. As soon as the door closed behind him Martin added, "You're trouble, Willis. You have been ever since you were a kid. It was you, the good Mormon, who got Moroni to try his first cigarette. And now that you work for the church you're even more dangerous. I can see it in your face."

Tanner spread his hands, palms up, a gesture of denial.

"If you've come here to hire Moroni, I'm advising him against it right now. I—" Martin's voice cracked. He coughed, wincing as he did.

"Hey, there's no problem, then. You and I are thinking alike."

"Never," Martin croaked.

"Sure we are. I'm here to do Mo a favor and relieve his workload, not hire him."

"That will be the day."

Traveler jumped in. "Willis is here because I asked for him. We need his help on our new case."

Tanner tried to smile but his squint returned, distorting the effort. "No can do, Mo. I'm here to save you time and trouble. Heber Armstrong is church business pure and simple."

"That's our missing missionary," Traveler explained for his father's benefit.

"We have the manpower to find him. You don't."

"What's wrong with one more person looking?" Traveler asked.

"Make that two," his father said.

"The church takes care of its own. You know that."

"We have a client," Traveler said. "A contract."

"Now, Mo. You know how the church works. If we have problems, we handle them quietly, without fuss or publicity. We can't have a few bad apples spoiling it for the rest."

"The Heber Armstrong I'm talking about seems to have been the ideal missionary. He set some kind of record for converting baseball players. Or so I've been told."

Martin cleared his throat. "Hold on. Your friend said bad apples. Plural."

"Did I?"

Martin grunted. "You'd better call your Tongan back in here, because I'm about to throw you both out on your asses."

"Take it easy, old man. I know my secrets are safe with you."

Tanner waved a hand at the door, where the Tongan's shadow could be seen through the frosted glass panel, before continuing in a whisper. "I admit it. We've got a short list of missionaries that we're concerned about. It's no big deal really. Like I said, we've got the manpower to take care of it. Take Buddy, for instance. We can red-shirt him and his kind as long as we need to."

Traveler leaned forward to stare his friend in the face. "Are you telling us that more than one missionary is missing?"

Tanner removed his glasses and placed them on the desk in front of him. Without the lenses his eyes looked vague, which was probably the effect he wanted. "I can't say anything like that. Not officially. I do God's work. It's a question of faith."

"My faith in you, or yours in mine?"

"Friendship is one thing, Mo, church business another. I hope you understand that."

"There's no other choice in this town."

"Fine. Then it's settled."

"I've been hired to find a missing person, Willis, as you so obviously know. Judging from what I've heard so far, it's probably a wild-goose chase. So why bother warning me off?"

"And if it isn't a wild-goose chase?"

"Then I'll have another satisfied client, won't I?"

Tanner studied his wristwatch in a deliberate manner. "You don't have a client. Newell Farnsworth will be calling here in fifteen minutes to terminate your services. I hope you've already cashed his check."

"And his daughter?"

"She's not your problem."

"What are you trying to cover up, Willis?"

"We're friends, Mo, so I don't like to say things like this. But you're not playing football in California now. This is Utah. Here some things count more than money."

"Which is one of the reasons I came back home."

"Listen to me. You're not a member of the church. I understand that. We're tolerant. Live and let live, that's our motto. But get in our way, Mo, and that's the end of you."

Tanner pushed back from his chair and stood up. "You know the rules. They're ours. We made them and we can change them any time we want."

Traveler shrugged.

"Just so we understand each other," Tanner said as he left the office.

Traveler immediately took the phone off the hook. "The man can't fire us if he can't reach us."

"You're better off out of it," Martin said before his voice cracked and he had to cough to clear his throat.

"Are you coming with me to Missing Persons or not?"

"Shit," Martin said, rising slowly to his feet. "Somebody's got to cover your back."

6

Fifty thousand years ago most of Utah was under water. Since then evolution and evaporation have taken their toll, leaving behind the Great Salt Lake as it is now, not to mention the vast desert sinkhole that became known as Brigham Young's promised land.

But there were times, like today, when Traveler got the feeling that God was trying to take it all back. A furnace wind, as astringent as the salt flats that spawned it, stung his eyes as he and his father fought their way to the parking lot.

Once there, they had to wrap handkerchiefs around their hands just to touch the car's door handles. But they couldn't keep the vinyl seats from scorching their backsides.

Squirming, Traveler said, "It must be a hundred and ten in here. I hope the air conditioner doesn't blow the engine."

"Don't you remember? A lizard of an old man like me doesn't need such things." Martin handed over his handkerchief so his son could grip the steering wheel with both hands.

The melting asphalt sang beneath the Ford's tires as Traveler headed down West Temple. When he turned left on Fourth South the car felt unstable, as if it were about to hydroplane.

Heat waves made the police building shimmer like a mirage on the verge of disappearing. Inside, a forty-degree drop in temperature made Traveler feel just as unstable.

Martin began shivering so badly his teeth clicked between words. "For Christ's sake. Let's go home. I'm getting too old for this kind of thing."

They found Sergeant Aldon Rasmussen, a sports fan turned dealer in sports memorabilia, on duty in Missing Persons. He led them past a counter meant to keep the general public at bay and into a cubicle surrounded on three sides by four-foot walls. It offered no privacy and only two chairs. Martin paced outside, trying to keep warm.

"I came across an old jersey of mine the other day," Traveler said by way of an opening ploy. An L.A. warm-up jacket had once paved the way for information on a runaway juvenile.

"Has it got your name and number on it?" the cop asked.

"Absolutely."

"What kind of condition?"

"There's still blood on it," Traveler lied.

"Yeah?" His eyes lit up. "What would you want for something like that?"

"Help with a missing person."

Rasmussen rubbed a thumb and forefinger together as if savoring invisible money. Traveler suspected he already had a customer in mind.

"Give me the name of your subject? I'll run it through the computer."

"Armstrong. Heber Armstrong."

"Forget it. That's one name I don't have to punch in. I know it by heart. Strictly hands off. Those are the orders." He blew on his fingers before tucking them into his armpits.

Martin stopped pacing long enough to give Traveler an I-told-you-so look.

"What if I autograph the jersey?" Traveler said.

"You know me, Moroni. I'd like to do it. I'd also like to keep my pension."

"Why the secrecy?"

Rasmussen smiled crookedly and pointed toward the heavens, or maybe just the executive offices above.

"Just tell me one thing. Is Heber Armstrong the only name on your forbidden list?"

"What about the jersey?"

"It's yours for a slip of the tongue."

"Three names came down. I was told that all of them were out of bounds as far as the police department was concerned, no matter who filed the missing persons report."

"I know you, Aldon. You'd punch them into the computer just to see what came up."

"Maybe."

"I'm signing that jersey, don't forget."

"Shit. Don't tell anybody where you got this, but only one of those names was ever officially reported as missing. The report was withdrawn the same day, whatever the hell that means."

"Watch it," Martin warned. "We've got company."

Traveler stepped out of the cubicle in time to see Newell Farnsworth, escorted by a lieutenant, bearing down on them.

"I'm here to terminate your services," the man announced as soon as he was within range.

"This is Mr. Farnsworth," the lieutenant said to Rasmussen, ignoring Traveler and his father. "I'm turning him over to you, Sergeant. It concerns one of those special cases that were discussed earlier. Do you follow me?"

"Yes, sir."

Traveler introduced Martin and himself.

"I'm aware of your reputation," the lieutenant said. "Father and son. One mean for his size, and the other mean because of it. Now, Sergeant, if you'll escort these gentlemen to the other side of the counter where the public belongs."

"Mr. Farnsworth too?"

"I think Mr. Farnsworth will be quite happy to leave."

Farnsworth was nodding even before the lieutenant finished speaking.

"You heard the lieutenant," Rasmussen said as he spread his arms and began herding them toward the counter.

Once they were beyond the barrier, Traveler took hold of Farnsworth's arm. "How did you know where to find us?"

"Mr. Tanner called me from church headquarters."

Traveler exchanged a pained look with his father. There was only one way for Willis Tanner to know something like that. He'd had them followed.

"Some detectives we are," Martin said.

"Is that *the* Willis Tanner you're talking about?" Rasmussen asked.

Traveler nodded.

"Shit." The cop turned and fled back to his cubicle.

His lieutenant grinned and said, "I guess that leaves me to escort you gentlemen downstairs."

No one spoke in the elevator. As soon as they passed out through the metal detectors, Farnsworth offered to shake hands. "I'm sorry, Mr. Traveler. When I got that call there was nothing else I could do."

"You can have your check back. We haven't cashed it yet."

"I'm not here about the money. There's someone God would like you to meet. He's waiting for us outside."

7

The man sitting cross-legged on a small patch of grass near the main entrance looked totally relaxed, as if the blistering heat had nothing to do with him. He rose at their approach, showing a lean body encased in clothes that Traveler hadn't seen the likes of since visiting the Pioneer Museum. His shirt, a pullover without buttons or collar, was made of soft homespun cloth. Its sleeves were loose and rolled to the elbows. His black trousers had no fly in the front. He was rosy-cheeked and youthful-looking despite a wispy gray beard and sixty years of wear. His twinkling eyes kept Traveler from labeling his a bishop's face.

"This is Orson Pack," Farnsworth said. "I'd like you to shake hands with him."

The man's long, bony fingers were cool despite the heat. His grip was firm.

Farnsworth beckoned to Martin. "You, too, if you don't mind?"

Martin shrugged and shook hands. Pack held on a beat longer than necessary.

My God, Traveler thought. He wouldn't have believed it if he hadn't seen it with his own eyes, not in this day and age. Farnsworth had set them up to be judged by the touch of a faith healer.

Traveler glanced at his father. Martin nodded back to

show he knew the score. "Well now, what's the verdict? Do my son and I pass?"

Farnsworth's mouth fell open.

"We're not as naive as you might think," Traveler said.

Farnsworth started to say something, then appeared to think better of it. He deferred to Pack.

"Lucifer is not among us," the man said.

"Orson is Reformed," Farnsworth explained.

In the language of Mormon country, that meant he was a member of one of the offshoot sects that had broken away from the LDS church. Association with such a man could cost Farnsworth his position as bishop. Even his soul, if it came to excommunication.

"He's shaken hands with the devil before and bested him. He has the power of healing in his touch, too."

Pack thrust his hands behind his back as if to keep them out of harm's way. "'Lay your hands upon the sick, and they shall recover.' Doctrine and Covenants, gentlemen. *The Book of Mormon* as it was written, as it will always be. Scripture is not open to interpretation. It cannot be updated or modernized to fit the times, or the needs of the church. It is the word of God."

Martin coughed. "Which reformed group are you with?"

"We are called the Saints of the Last Day. God's chosen people on earth."

Utah was filled with such men. True believers who, unlike Traveler, went through life without being tortured by doubts.

"Where are your headquarters?" his father asked.

Pack unclasped his hands and touched Martin again, as if reassuring himself that he hadn't lost his knack. "We have a place near Kamas."

Martin looked as surprised as Traveler felt. The town of Kamas stood at the edge of the High Uinta Primitive Area, unforgiving country high enough in the Uinta Mountains to be classified as a semiarctic region. Not the kind of place one expected to find a religious sect, most of which were hand-to-mouth operations that had trouble feeding themselves, let alone coping with freezing temperatures all year around.

"I might visit you one of these days," Martin said.

Traveler blinked in disbelief.

"Now that you've passed our test," Pack said with a nod to Farnsworth, "we want you to continue searching for Heber Armstrong."

"You seem to forget that we were fired ten minutes ago," Traveler said.

Farnsworth gestured for attention. "I was given an order. As a bishop I obeyed. But that doesn't mean Uncle Orson can't ask you to help my daughter find happiness."

"You'd better think that over carefully. In this state even the banks don't have secrets from the church. If we cash your check, Willis Tanner will know it. He works directly for the prophet, Elton Woolley."

"We've thought of that. I'll mail you cash in the morning. When you get it, tear up my check."

"My father and I have already been followed," Traveler said. "Otherwise Tanner wouldn't have known where to find us. By now he probably knows about our meeting with Mr. Pack."

"Suzanne's happiness is at stake, Mr. Traveler. With Orson's help I've come to realize that's worth any risk."

"What about the risk to her?"

"She loves Heber. That's all that counts as far as she's concerned."

"All right. A missing missionary appeals to me, I'll admit that."

"Now just a damned minute," Martin said. "I want a moment alone with my son, if you two don't mind."

He pulled Traveler as far as the 4th South curb, distant enough to be out of earshot. "In this town there's one rule of survival. Don't stick your nose into LDS business."

"Willis owes me one."

"You know better than that. To him, you're nothing but a soulless gentile. You're going to hell and he's going to an exclusively Mormon heaven."

Traveler changed the subject. "How does Pack strike you?"

Martin fished out the handkerchief he'd loaned his son earlier and coughed into it. A rattling sound came from his throat. "He seems sincere enough to me."

"What do you say? Let's give it a day or two. If we haven't found the missing kid by then we can always reconsider."

"Count me out. This is one time you're on your own."

Traveler reached out tentatively, as if searching for devils of his own. "Since when have you been afraid of anything, even the church?"

"A man changes when he gets old. He—" A fit of coughing doubled him over.

"Jesus, Dad. Are you all right?"

Traveler was wondering what the hell to do when Orson Pack arrived and went down on his knees in front of his father. In one practiced motion, his fingers pressed together and his head bowed. An instant later both hands reached out to take hold of Martin.

Within seconds the coughing stopped.

"Take me home," Martin whispered.

Traveler sought explanation in Pack's face, but the man's eyes were closed.

"We'll watch over him while you get your car," Farnsworth said.

Ignoring the heat, Traveler ran all the way to the parking lot. As soon as he pulled up to the curb in front of the police building, Pack and Farnsworth helped Martin into the front seat. Until that moment, Traveler hadn't seen the blood on his father's handkerchief.

8

Through gestures Martin communicated the fact that he didn't want to talk. It might start him coughing again. But there was something in his expression that told Traveler there was more to it than that. Even so, they drove in silence to the house on First Avenue, a one-story pioneer relic complete with adobe walls two feet thick. The place was sandwiched between U Street on the west and Virginia to the east, which for some reason had escaped Brigham Young's lettering system. Though the sun was beginning to set, the temperature hadn't dropped more than a few degrees.

As soon as they were inside, still cool because of the adobe, Martin led the way into the kitchen where he dug a bottle of scotch from beneath the sink.

"Straight or with water?" he asked his son in a whisper.

"I'll pass for the moment."

"Suit yourself." Martin, who still held the stained handkerchief clenched in one fist, leaned against the sink and drank directly from the bottle.

Traveler watched in sick fascination as his father's Adam's apple bobbed repeatedly. He'd never seen Martin drink like that. He was obviously fortifying himself to say something that already scared the hell out of Traveler.

When Martin took his mouth from the bottle, sweat beaded his brow and upper lip. He coughed once, tentatively. When that didn't trigger another attack he put away his handkerchief and sighed.

"Come on," he said. "Let's go into the living room and talk." He carried the bottle with him.

They sat on reclining chairs. The newest one, covered in brown tweed, had been Traveler's gift last Christmas.

Martin kicked back, took a short pull at the bottle, and then handed it to Traveler. "You'd better have one for yourself, son. We're both going to need it."

Traveler winced and swallowed a mouthful of scotch, as much to ease the knot in his stomach as please his father.

"I've got a tumor in my throat," Martin said.

Traveler came out of his recliner so fast he spilled whiskey down the front of his shirt and slacks.

"For Christ's sake, be careful." Martin fished the bottle cap from his shirt pocket and held it out at arm's length. "That's the last bottle and I've got a long night ahead of me."

Stunned, Traveler accepted the offering. The word cancer grew inside him until his chest felt constricted. He had to force air in and out of his lungs, and even then he felt light-headed.

"Don't just stand there, screw it on."

Traveler stared down at his trembling fingers.

"Here," Martin said. "Let me do that before you spill the rest of it."

The tumor of fear expanded. Death came with it, a thought so ugly that Traveler shook his head violently to rid himself of it.

Oh, Dad, was all he could say, and that wasn't out loud. *You've always been there when I needed you. You bailed me out when I was drunk at seventeen. You saved my sanity when I crippled a man playing football.*

Martin rose far enough in his recliner to take the bottle and cap from his son's palsied hands.

"Doc Murphy doesn't know if it's malignant or not. That's why I'm going back tomorrow."

Somehow Traveler managed to speak. He was surprised that his voice sounded normal. "For a biopsy?"

Martin nodded. "I'll go in the hospital as an outpatient in the morning and be out sometime in the afternoon. Whatever the verdict, Doc says the damned thing has got to come out eventually."

When Traveler reached for his father's hand, Martin pretended to misread the gesture. "Wait your turn. I'm not through drinking yet." He unscrewed the cap and tilted the bottle.

Traveler turned and walked to the other end of the long living room, where he stood staring out through the French doors. His father's Jeep, which was parked on the other side of the glass, blurred through tears. God, what were the options? Surgery. Radiation. Chemotherapy. He was afraid to ask.

"Your mother once said I'd drink myself to death." Martin's voice squeaked with the strain of reaching across the room. "For years after that I was a teetotaler."

Traveler leaned his forehead against the glass, expecting it to be cool. It was hot enough to make him jerk back.

"I was a bad influence on you, she used to say. I'll bet she'd turn over in her grave if she knew you turned out to be a detective."

I always wanted to be like you, even after I learned you weren't my real father.

Between them, paternity was a subject never mentioned directly, but only alluded to. Genes, Martin contended, were overrated. Upbringing was what counted.

I know the truth of that every time I look at you.

Traveler rubbed his eyes. If he broke down so would Martin. Neither of them could stand that. He took a deep breath and let it out slowly, willing himself to relax. When his shaking hands wouldn't cooperate, he thrust them into his pockets and returned to his father's side. "I'll drive you to the hospital tomorrow and then stick around until you're ready to come home."

"Go take a look at yourself." Martin thrust the scotch bottle at his son. "You look awful. Worse than I feel, for God's sake. You ought to get drunk. That's what I intend to do."

"Dad, I—" Traveler drank to hide a fresh surge of emotion.

"I don't want you moping around the hospital all day tomorrow either."

"You can't drive yourself home after an operation."

"They're only slicing off a little piece. No big deal."

"You'll be groggy from the anesthetic."

"I've always wanted a ride in an ambulance. I might even pay extra and have them use the siren."

"If I don't drive you, I'll worry even more."

"Who asked you to? You've got a job to do."

"I thought you wanted me to get out of it."

"There have been times in my life when I envied Mormons. No matter what happens, the church is always there to comfort them." Martin tilted his head to one side as if listening for the echo of what he'd just said. "This is one of those times."

Traveler fled to his bedroom at the back of the house. The room hadn't changed in thirty-five years, which was as far back as he could remember. The walls were knotty pine, the floor covered with a linoleum patterned like wooden planks. The furniture, battle-scarred from childhood, was 1940s maple meant to resemble early American. Martin had kept everything intact until Traveler moved back last year. Only then did his father threaten to sell off everything as junk.

There were times in this bedroom when Traveler awoke in the night thinking he was a child again.

"Oh, Dad," he breathed.

Martin spoke right behind him. "I ought to charge you rent."

"Don't sneak up on me like that."

"A good detective needs ears like a cat. Now, about that rent."

Somehow Traveler managed to smile. His father was a master at changing the subject when he wanted to avoid confrontation.

"I could always move back in with Claire," Traveler said.

"Now there's a woman to equal to your mother, my late wife."

"Kary wasn't that bad."

"I wasn't always this short, you know. It was Kary who cut me down to size."

"If that was true, Claire would have turned me into a dwarf by now."

Martin swallowed a mouthful of scotch. "She called the other day."

"You didn't tell me."

"What the hell good would it have done?"

Traveler shrugged. "What did she want?"

"The same as usual. She said she was lost and needed a private detective to come find her. I offered my services, but she said she was only interested in the Angel Moroni."

With that, Martin turned and walked back down the hall. Traveler followed his father all the way out of the house and onto the front lawn. There Martin pointed the bottle, now half empty, at his son's Ford. "You're blocking the driveway. I might want to get out later."

"You shouldn't be going anywhere," Traveler said. "You should rest. Besides, you're in no condition to drive."

" 'There's time enough for that in the grave,' someone once said." Martin stepped over to his Jeep, a dark-gray, four-wheel-drive station wagon that was his pride and joy, and ran a hand along its fender. After a moment he stood back to admire the sticker that ran across the rear bumper: OLD AGE AND TREACHERY WILL OVERCOME YOUTH AND TALENT.

"Don't I wish," Martin said, and slid in behind the wheel. After a moment he patted the passenger's seat.

"You're not driving," Traveler said as soon as he was inside.

He started to roll down the window but his father said, "Leave it be for a while. I got chilled in the house."

The interior of the Jeep felt like an oven.

Martin stared through the windshield as if intent on the road ahead. "I thought I had a summer cold at first. A mild sore throat, nothing more. Then three days ago I went to the dentist to have my teeth cleaned. He was the one who spotted the growth at the back of my throat. I hate going to the dentist, you know that. I put it off a long time. Maybe there are other things I've put off too long."

As Martin spoke the heat inside the car seemed to dissipate. Gooseflesh climbed Traveler's arms.

"Have I ever told you about your mother and me?"

Traveler blinked his stinging eyes. He'd spent a lifetime waiting for such a revelation. And now, when Martin was about to break his own taboo, Traveler realized he didn't want to hear anything that might turn out to be a death-bed confession.

Martin handed over the scotch. "You're right. I'd better stop drinking if I'm going to drive."

"I'll drive you anywhere you want to go. You know that."

His father gulped a breath preparing to answer but started coughing instead. Then he couldn't stop. In desperation he climbed out and bent over at the waist, coughing until he retched.

In time he said, "That sure as hell sobered me up."

"I still don't think you ought to drive."

"I'm too shaky right now. But the first chance I get I'm going to visit old friends, starting with Miles Beecham."

"You haven't seen him in years."

"Miles and I go back a long way. We were in the war together."

"He's an advising elder to the Council of Seventy, for

God's sake." In the hierarchy of the Mormon Church, the Council of Seventy was only a rung below the Twelve Apostles and the president himself, God's living prophet on earth.

He stared into his father's pleading eyes. What he saw there made him cringe.

Martin quoted from *The Book of Mormon*. "'Lay your hands upon the sick and they shall recover.'"

9

Traveler was in his bathrobe drinking coffee when someone cranked the old-fashioned doorbell at six-thirty the next morning. The man standing on the porch had the carefree face of an elderly cherub.

"Don't tell me," Traveler said. "You have to be Miles Beecham."

"That's right. And you're Moroni. I haven't seen you since you were a boy." He eyed the cup of coffee in Traveler's hand and shook his head in good-natured disapproval.

"Come in."

Beecham wore a gray suit that was tailored to hide most of his Santa Claus stomach. His twinkling blue eyes matched his tie and his short snow-white hair shone like a halo.

When he stepped across the threshold his nose twitched. Traveler had seen the maneuver before: good Mormons testing for cigarette smoke.

Beecham let out a sigh of relief. "I seem to remember that your father used to go against the Word of Wisdom."

Traveler had been thinking the same thing all night, wondering if cigarettes had caused Martin's tumor. Martin had kicked the habit years ago and would have done so even sooner, he liked to say, but for the fact that smoking was his way of protesting religious oppression.

"Your father called last night. He's expecting me."

"This is the first I've heard about it."

"He asked me to drive him to the hospital."

Traveler studied Beecham carefully, looking for any sign of a crack in his cherubic face, a hint of what he and Martin might be up to.

"Your father and I have been friends for a long time," Beecham said.

"Why are you here so early? Dad's not due at the hospital until nine."

Beecham smiled away the question. "Did Martin ever tell you about me?"

"Only that you two were in the war together."

He nodded. "That's just like him. He's special, you know. A deep one. A man of integrity. One of the few gentiles I've ever trusted completely."

Traveler had trouble swallowing. The words sounded too much like an epitaph.

"He saved my life."

"How?"

Beecham closed his eyes to recapture the memory. After a moment one hand began touching his chest as if searching for a wound.

"My father never talks about the war," Traveler prompted.

Beecham's eyes opened. He nodded. "Please tell Martin I'm here."

"I don't think he's awake."

Beecham closed his eyes again.

Shaking his head in wonder, Traveler trudged halfway down the hall to his father's room. Martin was sitting on the edge of his bed, fully dressed and waiting. He, too, wore a suit and tie.

10

Traveler took his time showering and dressing, but it was still too early to go to work. Fixing breakfast didn't appeal to him so he drove downtown and parked on Broadway, the name for Third South when it had been department store row. The street signs still said Broadway, but the department stores were gone.

He started walking but couldn't escape the haunting image of Martin dressed in suit and tie. Morticians dressed their clients like that.

Traveler shook his head. It wasn't like him to be morbid. But a suit and tie were so out of place in weather like this.

Think about something else, he told himself. Think about breakfast. And that's when he found himself standing in front of a grimy store window displaying used furniture that looked more abandoned than salable. Memory had led him to what was once the Broadway Café, a hangout of his youth.

Reversing direction, he headed for State Street. At the corner he paused in front of the Center Theater to look up and down the street, searching for targets of opportunity. Halfway up the block he spotted Wainwright's, known for its homemade doughnuts and pies. When he got there, a sign on the door said the place was going out of business in two weeks.

It was the same up and down that entire section of State Street. Even the old I & M Rug Company across the street, a fixture since the Great Depression, had been converted into a mall for antique stores.

Once seated at Wainwright's counter, Traveler had the impulse to order hundreds of doughnuts. They could be kept frozen for years, to be defrosted on those occasions when nostalgia got the better of him.

But he settled for two chocolate doughnuts, both of which he dunked. He was just finishing up when someone down the counter said, "Foreign money is ruining our town."

"Arab?" his neighbor asked.

"No. It's California money I'm talking about."

"Bull. It's the Japs you've got to worry about."

They were still arguing when Traveler left. By the time he walked the block and a half to his car, he was soaked with sweat.

He risked the air conditioner all the way to the fair grounds on North Temple and Eleventh West, which was also headquarters for the State Motor Vehicle Division. There, Judd Hatch left the line of limp-looking applicants to fend for themselves and treated Traveler to a cup of vending-machine coffee.

"I'm on my break," Hatch said to someone who glared at him. "Come on, Mo. We'll talk in the lunch room."

As soon as they were seated facing one another across a Formica-topped table, Hatch grinned and held his cup out in a toast. They touched cardboard rims.

"Every time I see you, Mo, I think of that South High game. That was the first time I broke my nose playing football. It's never been the same since."

"I remember. There was blood everywhere."

Hatch fingered his nose. "If it hadn't been for you, all of it would have been mine. Nobody else on our team raised a finger to help."

At six six, two hundred and eighty-five pounds, Hatch

had been the biggest kid at East High. In those days size was enough to get him on the football team.

"I was closest, that's all."

"You got kicked out of the game for breaking the other guy's nose."

"He sucker-punched you."

"But the referee didn't see it."

The refs hadn't seen much around Hatch. He was too awkward and too fat. As a lineman he was used more as an obstacle than anything else. He became the butt of jokes. But Traveler knew how he felt. Sudden spurts of growth had made him feel awkward and ungainly, too, particularly with girls.

"You were the only friend I had on that team," Hatch said.

"You're imagining things."

"Am I? I ran into Gus Evans a couple of weeks ago. You remember him, our great running back. Used to snap towels and play grab-ass in the showers."

Traveler nodded.

"The bastard asked me if I still had breasts."

Not a smart thing to do, Traveler thought. Since high school, Hatch had discovered weight-lifting. The flab of youth had been replaced by two hundred and sixty pounds of muscle.

"What did you say to him, Judd?"

"He was with some woman so I kissed him right on the mouth. Jesus Christ, you should have seen him. I thought he was going to puke on the spot."

"You keep doing things like that and you're going to lose your job. Then who will I have to run license plates for me?"

Hatch snorted. "The same old Mo. Come on. Let's find us a computer terminal."

They went down a long, linoleumed hall, trying one duplicate door after another until they found an empty office. When Hatch sat down the desk chair sighed desperately. "Let's have the number, Mo."

"I've only got a name this time. Heber Armstrong."

"What do you need?"

"I want to know if he has a current driver's license. If not, has he applied for one?"

"That's easy." Hatch entered his access code before typing out the name.

The computer beeped.

"His file's been flagged," Hatch said.

"What does that mean?"

"Any number of things. Too many tickets. Driving under the influence. A felony accident."

"Can you pin it down?"

Hatch pursed his lips. "I think I'll play this one cute and use someone else's access code."

"How can you do that?"

"Trade secrets."

Hatch typed in a combination of numbers and letters.

"Jesus, Mo. Look at this." He tapped the computer screen with his fingernail. "All inquiries concerning Armstrong, Heber, are to be directed to this telephone number. Now *that* is unusual."

Traveler agreed. The number belonged to Willis Tanner.

11

Brigham Young waved, or appeared to, as Traveler drove through the shimmering heat waves and passed the prophet's statue at the head of Main Street. Traveler intended to camp out in the lobby of what used to be the Hotel Utah until Willis Tanner granted him an audience.

But when he tried to pull into the underground parking lot a uniformed city policeman, not one of the usual security guards, waved him on his way.

Traveler switched off the car's radio and air conditioner and rolled down his window. "I'm here on business, officer."

"I'm sorry, sir. Visitors' parking is full."

"Willis Tanner," Traveler said, hoping the name might work miracles.

"I don't care who you are, sir. I have my orders." A second policeman arrived as backup.

Traveler saluted and drove the two blocks to his usual parking lot. Walking back would be hell. The radio had just told him so. As of 10:45 A.M. the temperature in Temple Square stood at one hundred degrees. A high-pressure area was centered over Utah. As long as it stayed put, the heat wave would continue.

The parking lot attendant had his radio on, only it wasn't reporting weather. A woman had been found murdered, this time in Jordan Park. Police were saying there were similarities with yesterday's killing. Both deaths had occurred on the west side of town. Salt Lake's real money lived on the east side.

By the time Traveler had walked back to the Hotel Utah, two more uniformed police officers were visible directing traffic. Another stood outside the entrance but didn't say a word when Traveler pushed through the door. Once inside, he felt as if he'd walked in on a missionaries' convention. Young men wearing suits were everywhere. They moved in and out of doors, up stairways and down, and back and forth across the lobby. But no one was waiting at reception.

Traveler approached warily. Today there were two young men behind the desk, each with his own computer terminal.

Traveler nodded at first one and then the other. "I'd like to see Willis Tanner."

"Is he expecting you, sir?"

Traveler thought that over. "Probably."

"Name, sir?"

"Moroni Traveler."

His angel's name caused the young men to exchange speculative glances before typing queries into their computers. Both looked surprised at the answer they got. Only one of them said, "I'll have you escorted upstairs, sir."

Two more young men materialized at Traveler's side. These two were Tongans, whose matching suits emphasized their bulk.

"If you'll please follow them, sir."

Traveler thanked the receptionists and accompanied his escorts, one of whom stayed behind him all the way. Tanner's office was on nine, the floor directly beneath the penthouse where Elton Woolley lived.

One of the escorts knocked and then stepped back, a practiced move. Their adherence to procedure reminded Traveler of his days on the L.A. police force, when he and his partner had knocked on dangerous doors.

Tanner opened the door and gestured impatiently at the Tongans to wait outside. Then he grabbed Traveler by the arm and attempted to pull him across the threshold. Traveler resisted just long enough to let his friend know who had the muscle.

The moment Tanner slammed the door he jabbed a finger in Traveler's chest. "You never listen, do you, Mo? I'm your friend. All I wanted was your cooperation. But what do I get? You playing games with motor vehicle records."

"Are you sure it was me?"

Tanner's face twitched as he fought to keep his squint in check. When he attempted another finger jab, Traveler caught hold of his hand and knocked it aside.

Stepping quickly, Tanner skirted his document shredder and retreated behind his desk. "Let me tell you something, Moroni. Hackers may be stealing atomic secrets from the government, but nobody messes with the church. That's gospel."

"Gospel according to St. Willis?"

"Go ahead. Make jokes. But your friend Judd Hatch isn't laughing. He's been suspended from his job pending a civil service review. His future is in your hands. If you do as you're told, I'll see that he's reinstated. Otherwise . . ." Tanner drew a finger across his throat.

To hide his anger, Traveler sat in the chair facing the desk and folded his arms. "I still want to know why you're making such a fuss about a missing missionary."

"That's not the point. You're prying into church business."

"His fiancée has a right to know what happened to him."

"Does she?" Tanner swung around in his chair and stared out the window. His office was on the west side, looking down on the temple. "Do you know what I see, Mo?"

Traveler said nothing. He knew a rhetorical question when he heard one.

"I can see all the way to the Hill Cumorah."

The Hill Cumorah lay in western New York state,

where the Angel Moroni revealed the golden plates of Mormonism to Joseph Smith in 1823.

"A blink and I see Nauvoo where we built our first temple."

Tanner tilted his head to one side, giving the impression that his vision was much more complex than that. When he turned around his eyes glistened, either with tears or inspiration, Traveler couldn't tell which.

"When a missionary is called," Tanner said, "he belongs to us. Not to the woman he leaves behind. Not even to his parents. For the next two years he is an ordained minister with the authority to baptize, conduct funerals, and marry members of our faith. But foremost he is a teacher, sworn to reveal our principles. Faith in Jesus, repentance, and the baptism of fire. Simple enough, wouldn't you say?"

Again Traveler knew better than to interrupt.

"Doctrine and Covenants, Mo. 'And to confirm those who are baptized into the church, by the laying on of hands for the baptism of fire and the holy ghost.'"

"I want to find Heber Armstrong, not destroy his faith."

"He was honored. Do you understand that? Joseph Smith sent out his first missionaries in 1837. And where do you think they went? England, of course. Heber Armstrong was following in their sacred footsteps. Brigham Young himself went to England on a mission in 1840. In the next two decades, seventy-five thousand were converted to the church."

"What you say has nothing to do with the fact that he's missing."

"You're my friend, Mo. I don't want this to get out of my control."

"You make that sound like a threat."

Tanner held a finger to his lips and then ripped a sheet of paper from a notepad on his desk. He placed the paper on a piece of glass before writing on it. As soon as he finished, he held it up for Traveler to read the single, scrawled word: *Danites.*

A secret society had been formed in the early days of the church. It was known under various names, the Brothers of Gideon, the Daughters of Zion, the Sons of Dan, or simply the Danites. They were said to have sworn a blood oath to the prophet, though the blood spilled invariably belonged to critics of the church. Present-day teachings said the Danites were nothing but myth, then and now.

Tanner shredded the paper.

"You've known me a long time, Willis. I'm not out to embarrass the church. All I want to do is help a young woman get married."

"It's me you're talking to, so let's stop fencing around. You smell blood and want in like everyone else."

"For God's sake. What the hell are you talking about?"

Tanner's jaw fell open. His eyes widened, as if looking for damage caused by the utterance of such obscenities. He pointed toward the penthouse. "My instructions come from the highest authority. Do you understand me?"

"Elton Woolley," Traveler mouthed silently.

"Exactly."

"I'm listening."

"These murders are off limits to you."

Traveler blinked in surprise.

Tanner sprang out of his chair. "You didn't know, did you?"

"I still don't."

Tanner's teeth snapped as he clenched his jaw. His Adam's apple bobbed, giving the impression that he was swallowing an obscenity of his own. He lurched around the desk to whisper in Traveler's ear. "I've vouched for you myself. My career is on the line."

"I didn't ask you to," Traveler whispered back.

Tanner mouthed, "Please."

"I want an explanation," Traveler said out loud.

With a sigh Tanner stretched out his hands and turned

them palms up. "'Shed my blood that I may be saved,'" he said, quoting Brigham Young.

According to Mormon gospel, horrendous crimes could be forgiven only by the shedding of the sinner's blood. There were times when Traveler believed in such a doctrine of blood atonement, but for different reasons.

12

The thermometer in direct sunlight outside the Chester Building was obviously broken. Either that or the city was about to reach the ignition point.

Traveler pushed through the bronze revolving door and breathed a sigh of relief. The building, faced with Wasatch Mountain granite on the outside and Italian marble on the inside, was a fortress against the heat.

Mad Bill was lying on the marble floor being fanned by Charlie Redwine, while Barney Chester and the two missionaries Traveler had seen yesterday looked on. Bill had exchanged his T-shirt for one of his ankle-length robes. A sandwich board proclaiming THE LOST TRIBE OF ISRAEL IS STILL LOST stood propped against the nearest wall.

"I told him not to go out in the sun dressed like that," Barney said. "But would he listen?"

Bill opened one eye and then the other. "Arabs do it. Besides, my disciple must be protected from the evils of proselytizing."

Charlie grinned.

"I could use a drink," Bill added.

When no one else made a move, Traveler hurried over to the cigar stand. Barney kept a jug of cheap red wine hidden under the counter for emergencies, which both Bill and Charlie contrived to effect on a daily basis.

Bill sat up to receive the offering that Traveler had poured discreetly into a coffee cup. Each time Bill swallowed, Charlie licked his lips in vicarious pleasure. But the missionaries had eyes only for Traveler, which made him wonder if they'd been sent by Willis Tanner.

"They've been following me and Charlie all day," Bill said, rising slowly to his feet with the Indian's help. "We were visiting the Era Antique Shop to collect our tithing when God spoke to me."

"They were stealing," one of the missionaries clarified.

"He told me to don my sandwich board and spread the word. Charlie, my Lamanite, must be secure from the likes of them. Do you realize that I barely got out of that place without having to pay?"

From beneath his robe Bill produced an old photo album, covered in faded brown velvet and trimmed in brass scrollwork. "Take a look at this, Moroni." He pointed out the price tag. "I have parishioners just waiting to pay a ten percent tithe on the dollar."

The tag said $100. Traveler took out a ten-dollar bill and handed it to Charlie. "Your ransom is paid. Now take it back and tell them it was a mistake."

"We haven't looked inside yet," Bill complained.

"The price stays the same."

Bill shrugged and began thumbing through the album while Traveler looked over his shoulder. Pioneer faces, stern and dark-eyed, stared from one oval frame after another. Halfway through the album Bill came upon an old postcard that had been cut to fit into one of the photo insets. The Coon Chicken Inn, a Salt Lake landmark torn down in the late 1950s, jumped out at Traveler and caught him in its time warp. The memory wasn't a pleasant one.

He'd been eight, maybe nine. For him, walking into the Coon Chicken was always the best part. The door was a bright white tooth, set in a grotesque smile that belonged to a thirty-foot-high caricature of a black man. One of his eyes was winking, an invitation to try his famous fried chicken and biscuits.

Traveler's father made it a point to wink back. "One of these days," Martin said, "those teeth are going to snap someone right in two."

"What the hell is that supposed to mean?" Traveler's mother asked.

Martin shrugged. "You tell me, Kary."

"You think I'm stupid, don't you?"

"Don't start. We came here to have a good time."

"Me? You're the one with the big mouth."

"I'm sorry."

"Saying something like that could frighten the boy."

Traveler shook his head to deny any such thing. The Coon Chicken Inn was his favorite restaurant. No place else was like it. Inside was all knotty pine and red leather booths. It even had a bandstand and dance floor, though the latter wasn't much bigger than a desktop. Above all, it had black waiters who looked like the face outside. The only other black men Traveler had ever seen were porters at the train station.

A white hostess showed them to a booth.

The grinning, trademark face was repeated on the menus. When their waiter arrived he grinned, too, and even winked.

"Who the hell are you smiling at?" Kary demanded.

"Just the boy, ma'am." The waiter ducked his head and seemed to shrink. Even so, he was the tallest man Traveler had ever seen.

Traveler slid down in the booth until his head was at table level.

"I think we know what we want," Martin said.

"Don't rush me," Kary exploded.

The waiter started to back away.

Kary glared at Martin and then the waiter. "I don't like the way he's looking at me. Showing those big buckteeth of his. You said it yourself, Martin. He's just looking for someone to bite."

"Now, Kary."

"A white woman shouldn't have to put up with that."

Martin shook his head at the waiter to apologize.

"You're the goddamned war hero," Kary shouted. "You ought to be able to handle a nigger, no matter how big he is."

Traveler reached over Bill's shoulder and turned the album page to escape the memory. A yellowed newspaper clipping fluttered to the floor. Bill pounced on it, his heat stroke forgotten.

"An omen," he announced as soon as he unfolded the disintegrating paper. He held it out at arm's length.

It was from one of those supermarket tabloids. The headline said: Your Co-worker Could Be a Space Alien.

Bill retracted his arms and began to read out loud. "Here's how you can tell. One: Watch for odd or mismatched clothes."

He eyed the missionaries up and down, looked disappointed, and went on. "Two: Strange diet or unusual eating habits."

Bill shook his head. "Three: Bizarre sense of humor. Space aliens who don't understand earthly humor may laugh during serious moments or tell jokes that no one else understands."

As if on cue one of the missionaries giggled.

Bill's arm stretched out, his forefinger pointing like Michelangelo's God about to touch Adam. "Mormons are from outer space. There's no other explanation."

Traveler held out his hand, palm up.

Reluctantly Bill surrendered the clipping. Traveler tucked it back into the album, which he then gave to Charlie. "Like I said before, take it back."

Charlie glanced toward the cigar stand.

"He needs refreshment," Bill interpreted. "Especially in this kind of weather."

"How about a nice cold glass of water?" Barney asked.

Bill folded his arms. "Jesus turned water to wine. Should you do less?"

"I give up," Barney said, and headed for the jug, his steps dogged by Bill and Charlie. The missionaries stayed behind with Traveler.

"Will you join us, Moroni?" Barney called as soon as he was behind the counter.

"I've got work to do."

When Traveler reached the elevator he paused to look back at the missionaries. They were whispering like spies who wanted to follow him upstairs but didn't have the nerve.

13

Traveler called home, got no answer, and then tried the LDS Hospital. The Outpatient Clinic confirmed that his father had been there for tests but had already been released.

He decided to see Dr. Murphy in person, walking the four blocks to the Boston Building on Exchange Place despite the heat. Murphy's office had air conditioners providing enough cross-ventilation to keep the temperature in the low seventies. As a result the doctor wore his usual gray herring-bone sports coat and charcoal slacks. His tie was regimental English, his tasseled loafers Italian, his outlook strictly parochial. He'd been a friend for years.

He rubbed his bald head before shaking Traveler's hand. The grip felt too firm, too deliberately reassuring. But he met Traveler's questioning stare without flinching.

Even so, a surge of fear soured Traveler mouth. He swallowed dryly and sat down. His old football coach, Bart Siddons, would have gotten a kick out of how badly Traveler's hands were shaking. "You're never afraid, are you?" Siddons used to say every so often during one of his locker-room talks. "You're reckless. You throw your body at people like you don't give a damn. Tell me honestly. Have you ever been afraid?" What the hell kind of question was that to ask a man in public?

Dr. Murphy, who'd moved behind his desk, came to

Traveler's rescue by speaking first. "There was no problem with the anesthetic or the biopsy. Martin came through that fine."

Traveler tried to nod but his neck muscles wouldn't budge.

"In most cases we get a preliminary culture reading immediately. It's not conclusive of course, but we can usually get a good idea about what we're dealing with, whether it's malignant or not. In Martin's case there was a difference of opinion, so more tests have to be run."

"When will you know for sure?"

"In addition to workups at the hospital, I've had samples sent to the university. The best medical research in the world is being done right here at home, you know. So I'd say two days. Three at the most. Certainly not long enough to make a difference."

"Did you look at the culture yourself?"

"Of course. I was standing right there beside the surgeon all the time."

Traveler held his breath. He'd been coming to Dr. Murphy since childhood and had absolute faith in the man's judgment.

"I'll tell you the same thing I did your father. I don't like it. I never do when I see anything that's out of the ordinary."

"What did the surgeon say?"

"That it looks operable. But it's in a bad location if it's malignant."

Traveler glanced down at his trembling, ice-cold fingers. "How did Dad take all this?"

"He had a friend with him. That always helps. An elder of the church."

"I know."

"I've known Martin a long time, perhaps too long to be able to keep any kind of professional distance. But one thing I do know. He's not the kind of man to give up without a fight."

The doctor came around his desk to hug Traveler. "Like father, like son, I always say."

Traveler fled before emotion got the better of him.

The sweltering heat of the Chester Building's third floor felt good at first. It warmed Traveler's fingers. But it took half a glass of whiskey to stop them shaking. Once they did, he picked up the phone and dialed the direct number to Missing Persons at the police building.

"This is Sergeant Rasmussen speaking."

"It's Moroni Traveler. Is your lieutenant listening in?"

"I've never heard of you. Besides, you're too big to be named for an angel."

"I need a little information."

"You're too late. Those computer files have been erased."

"Then you won't mind giving me what you have on that murder in Jordan Park."

"Call homicide, for Christ's sake."

"I don't know any football fans there."

"Hold on, Traveler. Let's keep everything straight between us. I'm a businessman, not a fan."

"I've still got my old helmet." At least so he hoped. Everything, including a couple of helmets, had been shipped home for storage after his early retirement from football. He'd never asked Martin what he'd done with the stuff but, knowing him, it was probably stored away carefully somewhere.

"The one you wore in the Super Bowl?"

"It's got the dents to prove it."

"What the hell do you want, my right arm?"

"Everything you can give me on the murders."

"It ain't much. Even so, it'll be my ass if somebody finds out I've been talking to you."

"I'll take whatever you've got."

"And the helmet is mine, no matter what?"

"I'll bring it to your office myself."

"No fucking way. You mail it to my house. I don't want to be seen with you."

"It's a deal."

"I can give you a name. That's all."

"I'm listening," Traveler said.

"Maria Gomez. And one more thing. You'll need a goddamned lawyer to see her."

14

Reed Critchlow called himself a philosopher and chronicler of local history. He'd been a tenant of the Chester Building for forty years, long enough to observe its evolution from one of Salt Lake's more fashionable addresses to near-derelict and back again, to its present nostalgic elegance.

He was Martin's age and, like Martin, semiretired when it suited him. His legal advice had kept Traveler out of jail on more than one occasion. His office, at the opposite end of the hall from Moroni Traveler & Son, had a western exposure, looking out at the Great Salt Lake and the Oquirrh Mountains, masked in blue-gray haze from the copper smelters. The furniture was pioneer pine, battered and scarred. But his law books were up to date.

"I know that look of yours, Moroni," he said from behind his desk. "At this stage in my life I don't need the kind of troubles you attract."

"It goes with the job, Martin always says. Yours and his."

"Both of us should have been put out to pasture years ago."

Traveler smiled grimly. "Have you spoken with my father in the last couple of days?"

Critchlow sprang out of his chair like a young man. "Your tone tells me he's in trouble. Whatever it is, I'm ready to help."

"There's nothing either of us can do."

"Come on, Mo. I've known you since you were small enough to spank."

Traveler hesitated. If Critchlow, one of Martin's oldest friends, hadn't been informed about the tumor, then it wasn't Traveler's place to do it.

"We've got a difference of opinion concerning the case I'm on," Traveler said. "Martin would like me to drop it. Unfortunately I can't because someone else has threatened me if I don't."

Critchlow sank back into his chair and propped his feet up on the desk, sighting at Traveler between his wing tips. "If it's advice you need, fine. Just so I don't have to go out in this damned heat."

His casement-mounted air conditioner, located in the outer office where his part-time secretary worked, was fighting a losing battle against glass-intensified sunlight coming in through the western window.

"It could be murder," Traveler said.

Critchlow shifted his feet, sat up straight, and lit one of the cigars he and Barney Chester had in common. "I haven't had a murder case in years. Who's our client?"

"That's the problem. One minute I'm looking for a missing missionary and the next thing I know Willis Tanner is claiming church prerogative and talking about murder. It's something to do with those two women who've been killed."

"Goddamn," the attorney said, his eyes lighting up. "Jack the Ripper and Mormons. I love it."

Traveler quickly summarized the situation, concluding with the name he'd been given by Sergeant Rasmussen, Maria Gomez. Critchlow fired smoke rings at an upraised finger. "All we need now are polygamists."

"One last thing," Traveler said. "I'm here because my contact at the police department said I'd need a lawyer."

"Why?"

"That's the problem. I don't know."

"What do you want from me then?" Critchlow asked.

"Your company at the police station."

Critchlow stepped inside the police building, took one look around, and said, "I've been coming here, or places like it, damn near every day of my life. So they can't fool me. Something very strange is going on."

"A maniac's killing women," Traveler reminded him.

"I've been through worse." The lawyer's head swiveled from side to side as he studied the mix of people in the main lobby. Traveler did the same. Considering the location, the college-age men in suits were more likely to be federal agents than missionaries.

"See anybody you know?" Critchlow asked.

A 250-pound Polynesian, much like the ones surrounding Willis Tanner, was standing next to the metal detector. Traveler pointed him out and explained his sudden preoccupation with Tongans.

"You stay here. I'll check him out," Critchlow said.

The lawyer struck up a conversation with one of the uniformed officers supervising the security checkpoint. Judging by the back-slapping generated, they knew one another. The cop even let Critchlow borrow his phone.

The attorney returned after a lengthy, somewhat animated conversation. "Your man is with the feds, supposedly here as an observer, but nobody knows what he does exactly."

"Maybe I've got Tongans on the brain."

"Forget about him. I was right. All hell is breaking loose. I've had to call in some markers just to get us inside to see the Gomez woman. Even then, we may need the ACLU before this is over. The story they're putting out is that she's an illegal alien who's being held until the Immigration people get here. But if that were the case, I wouldn't have had to spend favors. From now on stick close and keep your mouth shut until I say otherwise. Let them think you're a colleague I've brought along as a consultant. Remember, in all likelihood we've only got a few minutes before word gets out and the shit hits the fan."

"I hope you know what you're doing," Traveler said. In slacks and pullover shirt he looked like anything but a lawyer.

Critchlow led the way to a holding area Traveler had never seen before. By jail standards, the cells were spacious and the usual antiseptic smell was missing. A small table with two facing chairs was set up in the linoleumed corridor outside the cells.

"I'm here to represent Maria Gomez," Critchlow told the female jailer who met them.

She nodded. "The front desk called to say you were on the way."

When she turned to open the cell door, the lawyer winked at Traveler.

The woman inside the cell was very young, no more than seventeen or eighteen, and still wearing her own clothes, faded jeans that were baggy around the knees and tennis shoes that looked like Goodwill hand-me-downs. Her dark, Indian skin faded when she moved under the corridor's bright fluorescent lights. Despite disheveled hair and red, swollen eyes, she had a serene beauty about her. But that gave way to fear when Critchlow spoke. "I'm an attorney, Maria. I'm here to help you."

Her pleading eyes looked at the jailer, whose only answer was to point at one of the chairs. When Critchlow pulled it away from the table, Maria eyed him warily as if suspecting trickery instead of politeness.

"Sit down," he said. "Please."

Her eyes turned to Traveler.

"We're both here to help you," Critchlow assured her.

She sat. "I have no money to pay you." She surprised Traveler by speaking without an accent.

"Everyone is entitled to a lawyer whether they can pay or not." Critchlow slipped into the chair across from her. The jailer walked far enough away to be out of earshot, but still close enough to keep an eye on all three of them.

"I was told not to talk to anyone." Her eyes went to the jailer.

"Anything we say here is privileged information," Critchlow said. "Do you understand?"

"I watch television. I know about the law. That's why I want to be a citizen, too." Her eyes glittered. "I wanted to do what's right. But I should have known better. Rosie warned me but I wouldn't listen." She blinked tears.

"Who's Rosie?"

"She's my friend. We were walking to catch the bus this morning, on our way to Federal Heights where we do housework."

Federal Heights, high in the foothills east of the Avenues, was old money and mansions. Originally it had been the bastion of Salt Lake's richest nonconforming families, Catholics, Presbyterians, and Baptists seeking sanctuary from the omnipresent LDS. The Heights, it was said, guaranteed asylum because of its proximity to Fort Douglas, a federal garrison positioned on high ground in the late nineteenth century as a reminder to Brigham Young that polygamy would no longer be tolerated.

"These people you work for in Federal Heights, did they pay for you to come into the country?"

She nodded. "Five years ago."

"You were only a kid," Traveler blurted.

"Mo," Critchlow warned without taking his eyes from the woman. "Now, Maria, these people you work for, what are their names?"

"They've been good to me. They let me watch TV. That's how I learned to speak English. I don't want to get them in trouble."

"What about Rosie then?" Critchlow persisted. "How can we find her?"

Maria shook her head. "Times are bad. I see that on television. There are people who have no money at all, no jobs, and no place to live."

"We'll find her sooner or later."

Her eyes narrowed. "How?"

"You said that you and Rosie both work in Federal Heights."

She nodded warily.

"We can search every house if necessary if you don't talk to us."

Maria closed her eyes and made the sign of the cross. "Every day we leave very early, when it's just starting to get light. It's shorter if we walk across the park. That's where we saw the body. Rosie told me it was none of our business. But I couldn't walk away and leave that poor girl lying there. She was naked. I kept thinking that children might come along and find her like that. So I called the police like they tell you to on TV."

She sighed and opened her eyes. "Now they say they're going to keep me locked up here until the INS decides what to do with me."

"Bullshit," Critchlow said, turning to Traveler. "Having illegals as housemaids in Federal Heights is a status symbol. Everybody looks the other way. So why the hell are they playing games with Maria?"

Until recently illegals weren't all that common in Utah where the church, through its vast missionary program, was able to recruit cheap labor. But such converts, even the most zealous, become citizens sooner or later. After that, they wanted decent wages like everyone else.

Critchlow scratched his head hard enough to produce dandruff. "There's only one explanation I can think of."

Traveler had thought of it, too.

"You and Rosie must have seen the killer."

"No," Maria said, but her voice betrayed her. She'd seen something.

Critchlow reached out to comfort her. Down the corridor the jailer came to attention.

The lawyer removed his hand. "Help us, Maria."

A door slammed in the distance. It sounded like the same one Traveler and Critchlow had come through to reach the holding area.

"Tell us," Critchlow urged.

"I'd seen the dead woman in the neighborhood before. I think she was a prostitute."

"Her name?"

"I don't know."

"Her friends?"

Maria shook her head in ignorance.

"What then?"

Her eyes dropped.

Another metal door opened and closed. Footsteps were coming their way.

"How can I tell a man such things?"

"Please," Traveler said.

"There was a note sticking from her body." She looked at her own lap, shifting uncomfortably. "It was down there."

The final door opened. Traveler saw two uniformed officers, followed by two young men who could have been missionaries or agents.

Maria stared at the newcomers and whispered, "I didn't touch it. I didn't. Something was written on it in blood."

15

Critchlow went searching for someone who might be dumb enough to issue a writ for Maria Gomez, while Traveler got into line in the lobby to make a phone call. The man ahead of him looked familiar, but Traveler couldn't place him until he made his call. He was a reporter for the *Tribune*.

"They've clamped the lid on here," he said. "Some lawyer beat me to it and they've decided to move her. Where? If I knew that, I'd be there, wouldn't I? What I've got is rumor, not even a goddamned informed source if you ask me. At the moment my guess is she's some kind of material witness. An illegal. If they really want to get cute, they could ship her out of the country on the next plane. I heard someone suggest it. Mexico, Guatemala, someplace like that. I don't know for sure."

Traveler tapped the man's shoulder.

"In a minute," the reporter snapped without bothering to look at the detective. Into the phone he said, "Not you. Some clown wants the phone."

Traveler tapped again, this time harder. The man swung around, his free hand thrust out in a fist. When he saw the size of Traveler, he unclenched his fingers and waved them to show he meant no harm.

"I've got to hang up now," he said into the phone. "Sure, sure. I'll call as soon as I get anything."

Smiling apologetically, he cradled the receiver.

"I heard you say something about a woman being sent out of the country."

Obsequiousness gave way to immediate suspicion. "Are you with the *Deseret News?*"

"I'm a private detective."

"Sure," the man said, and fled in the direction of the nearest uniform.

Traveler dialed his office. Martin answered so quickly he must have been right next the phone.

"I could use some help," Traveler told him.

"What is this, therapy to keep the old man busy?"

"You're the one with the contacts at the Federal Building."

"Are you still after the missionary?"

"That's the way it started out."

"The feds don't worry about missionaries, except maybe the State Department."

"Something's going on with a woman named Maria Gomez. She's an illegal who found the body of that woman in the park, and now there's talk of deporting her for it."

"What the hell am I supposed to do?"

"Ask around. Find out what the INS plans to do. Will there be a formal hearing before they send her back? That kind of thing."

"I'll do it in the morning."

"And if they ship her out tonight?"

"Come on, Moroni. You know better than that. Those people never do anything in a hurry. Besides, I was about to leave for Kamas."

Traveler groaned inwardly. Orson Pack, the man who recognized devils by the touch of his hand, had said his Saints of the Last Day were headquartered there.

"For God's sake, Dad."

"Exactly."

Only a couple of days ago such a response would have been indicative of Martin's humor. Now the tone was wrong. In it Traveler heard desperation and fear. Or was that himself he was listening to?

"I'm an old man," Martin said. "Old men get cautious. They like to hedge their bets."

"With Orson Pack?"

"I know what you're thinking, that he's just another of Utah's religious screwballs. You could be right, but he seemed sincere to me."

"I've met a lot of lunatics who were quite sincere in their insanity."

There was a long pause. Traveler could hear the squeak of the desk chair as his father swung around to look out the window. Probably he was staring up at the Angel Moroni, their namesake.

Martin sighed. "All right. I'll make a couple of calls before I leave. Where can I reach you if I get anything?"

"I'm at the police building now, but you'd better leave me a note."

"Fine."

"Drive carefully, Dad."

"Sure."

When Traveler turned away from the phone, Critchlow was waiting for him. "It's out of my hands, Mo." The lawyer spread his fingers as if to prove the point. "There's nothing more to be done."

"What kind of bail have they set?"

"I may not go to Sunday School, but I'm still a member of the church."

Traveler blinked in surprise. "I smell something more than cigars on your breath."

"Originally I became LDS for my wife's sake."

"And now?"

"For her sake I have to walk away from this."

"Who got to you?"

Critchlow sighed and shook his head.

"You promised the Gomez woman that you'd help her."

"She's not really a suspect, so she doesn't need a lawyer."

"She's a victim. You know that as well as I do."

He ducked his head. "Come on. I've set something up for you. It's the best I can do. After that you're on your own."

"Look me in the eye and say that."

When Critchlow did as requested, Traveler saw no sign of guile. But then lawyers were like actors, reflecting truth to suit the occasion.

Traveler followed him past the metal detectors and down a long, first-floor corridor that ultimately led to the office of chief of police. They stopped in front of the chief's door and the lawyer knocked quietly, with a single knuckle.

Miles Beecham opened the door and smiled. "I'm glad you came, Moroni. We need to talk."

"What the hell is going on?"

Beecham thrust out a chubby hand in greeting. Traveler ignored the offering to glare at Critchlow, who half bowed at Beecham before walking away.

"Don't blame him, Moroni. He follows orders like the rest of us."

"And who's giving you orders?"

"Willis Tanner asked me to help. As a friend of the family I'm glad to do it."

"I understand. The church speaks and even the chief of police goes fishing."

"Not at all. I merely borrowed his office for a few minutes. Now, if you don't come inside and talk I'll be forced to have you arrested."

As a representative of the Council of Seventy, Beecham probably had the power to have the chief himself arrested.

"Why not? I like to talk," Traveler said, crossing the threshold as nonchalantly as possible.

The office reminded him of a movie set. Everything was on too large a scale: the walnut desk flanked by state and federal flags, the wall of photographs and plaques, the conference table, the richly upholstered chairs.

He took a seat. Beecham perched on the edge of the desk, giving him the advantage of height for the first time. "I'm here for one reason only, Moroni, to do what's best for you, just the way I did for Martin. I personally conducted a healing session for him this morning, which wasn't easy, I assure you. Normally such gatherings are reserved exclusively for the faithful."

"Are you claiming a cure?"

Beecham launched himself at Traveler, who resisted the urge to duck. The man grabbed hold of Traveler's shoulders; his fingers dug in.

"I laid hands upon your father. What happens now is up to God and the strength of Martin's faith."

"You've known him too long to believe something like that."

" 'Behold, I came into the world not to call the righteous but sinners to repentance.' Apt, wouldn't you say? The Book of Moroni, eight: eight, from *The Book of Mormon*."

"And what about Maria Gomez? Is she a sinner?"

"You and Brother Critchlow saw her. There's nothing to be done about that now."

"I don't understand your interest in this."

"The church is interested in everything. As an advisor to the Council, it's my job to bring men like Reed Critchlow back into the fold."

"He can take care of himself. Maria Gomez can't."

"I don't know what she told you, but the truth is she's being held here for her own protection. She's a witness. Her life could be in danger."

"She says she didn't see the killer."

"She's not one of us, Moroni. Not one of the Saints, not even a citizen. Those people aren't like us."

"Don't count me among your Saints."

"Yours is a pioneer family. You will always be one of us, willing or not. It's the outsiders we have to stand against. With them, with people like the Gomez woman, lying is a way of life."

Traveler snorted. "Too bad there's no mirror in here.

You ought to see your own face. It's better than a lie detector."

Beecham rubbed his ruddy cheeks as if to erase the evidence.

"Maria Gomez had no reason to lie about the murder. Or the note she saw, which, I gather, was stuck in the dead woman's vagina."

Beecham winced. "Pioneer Days are coming. We can't have things like that in the papers."

"I'm not interested in publicity."

"Nevertheless, I'm ordering you to disengage from this case."

"Exactly who are we talking about, Maria Gomez or Heber Armstrong?"

"Today's the twenty-first, Moroni. Seventy-two hours from now marks the date when Brigham Young first set eyes on our valley. 'This is the place,' he said. And it is, Moroni. It's ours and nobody can take it away from us."

"I love it, too."

Beecham's brow wrinkled. "What do you think Brigham Young would say to us? I ask myself that question all the time. Would he blame me for what's happened? Or the Council? Or the Apostles? Could we have done our jobs better and kept our missionaries from defecting?"

16

The sun was past its zenith and heading west toward the Great Salt Lake when Traveler left the police building. Seagulls, like the ones that had saved the first settlers' crops from locust, were cooling off under sprinklers set on random timers to keep street people from roosting on the grass. As Traveler watched a single bird took flight, followed almost immediately by the others. Their easy freedom made him wonder about his own. Miles Beecham wasn't the kind of man to make idle threats about jail.

Traveler looked around, saw no sign of being followed, and started walking. The heat had slackened off, or maybe he was getting used to it. But the Ford's metal skin was still hot enough to fry bugs, and the upholstery provided a thrill.

By the time he reached the Chester Building's parking lot, cool air had just started trickling from the air-conditioning vents. A long limousine with darkened windows was straddling his parking space. The attendant was nowhere to be seen.

Traveler pulled into a vacant space and was opening the door to get out when he saw the two men approaching his car, one blond, one brunette. He had the impression they'd come from the direction of the limousine. Both were big and rangy. He had twenty pounds on them. They had twenty years on him. Their staggering walk said they'd been drinking and were looking for trouble.

"Look what we've got here," the blond one said.

"A fucking football hero," his dark-haired buddy answered.

"They're all locker-room fags, Blackie."

They separated so they could come at Traveler from both sides. Their calculating eyes and precise movements spoiled the drunk act.

Traveler stole a quick look at the limo but the glass was impenetrable.

"Moroni Traveler," the blond spat out, making it sound like filth.

"Named for an angel," Blackie picked up. "But our schools weren't good enough for him. He had to go to USC."

They had the tough look of coal miners from Price, or maybe smelter workers from Bingham. Or even cops.

"If you're police, I want to see ID."

"You won't be seeing anything when we get through with you."

Traveler smiled. Whatever they were, they were amateurs. Professionals didn't brag.

Their loud talk had attracted a West Temple wino from behind one of the cars at the back of the lot. He held a brown-bagged bottle in one hand and was scratching his ass with the other.

Traveler's breathing changed, part of the psyching technique he used to get himself ready for football games. Coach Siddons had taught him how to do it. *Turn yourself into a psycho. It's the only way to survive. You've got the eyes already, Mo. The mad eyes of a linebacker.*

The blond moved first, without bothering to feint. Traveler took him out with a forearm to the throat and was turning to meet Blackie when the sharp edge of a shoe caught him on the thigh. His right leg went numb, collapsing him so suddenly the next blow missed. He caught the man's foot on the way by, yanked it, but didn't have the leverage to dislocate the joint.

Blackie rolled like a tumbler and bounced to his feet. Traveler climbed through pain to stand against him. He felt blood running down his leg where he'd hit pavement. His slacks were torn, an elbow skinned. The pins and needles torturing his right leg told him he might not be able to keep his feet against another attack.

But Blackie made a mistake. He didn't follow up. Instead, he stopped to look at his gagging partner who was writhing on the ground concerned with one thing only, sucking air through his damaged throat.

Traveler positioned himself carefully, keeping his right thigh out of the line of attack.

"I could have killed him if I'd wanted to," he said.

Blackie's eyes lost focus. He lunged like a berserker.

Traveler reacted insinctively, launching himself like a true linebacker. His shoulder rammed into the man's solar plexus. Air whooshed out along with a recent meal.

But Blackie surprised him. Though gasping for breath, he rolled out of reach and regained his feet. The look on his face said he wasn't through yet.

Traveler caught movement at the extreme edge of his vision. A viaduct derelict, pushing a wire supermarket basket filled with his belongings, had joined the wino. Traveler adjusted his head slightly to expand his field of vision. Beyond the pair a police car was cruising by, the officers inside obviously aware that a fight was taking place. They didn't stop.

Blackie grinned. "That's right, asshole. No one's coming to your rescue."

Traveler ground his teeth. This was Beecham's move, a setup. Those cops would keep circling the block until the fight was over. Win or lose, he was the one who'd be arrested. If he lost badly enough, bail would only get him out of jail and into the hospital.

His hands went ice cold despite the heat. He had two minutes, maybe less before the car came around again.

The blond was up on one knee, wheezing. The fight was just starting to come back into his eyes. Traveler broke his leg with a single kick. The snap of bone and the scream were almost simultaneous.

The wino cheered. Blackie's face grew old and tired in an instant. He held his hands up and began backing away.

One minute to go, Traveler reckoned, and limped toward the limousine. The engine roared just before the car lurched over the curb and out onto First West, where it stopped momentarily to pick up Blackie.

By then the blond's voice had given out. He was reduced to sobs.

Traveler left him to the police and got back into his own car and drove away. Half a minute later he parked in a loading zone in front of the Chester Building.

The lobby was empty. The only person on duty was Nephi Bates, the elevator man, who grinned openly at Traveler's battered appearance. Once Bates had closed the door, he ignored the operating mechanism and began thumbing through his *Book of Mormon*, which bristled with page markers.

"Ah," he said, finding his place. " 'The justice of God is the punishment of the sinner . . .' "

Traveler reached across to start the elevator himself.

" '. . . for ye do try to suppose that it is injustice that the sinner should be consigned to a state of misery.' "

By the time Traveler reached his office, his injured thigh had cramped so badly he was moving with a stiff-legged shuffle. His father, who was sitting at the desk writing, looked up and shook his head as if to say I told you so. "Do I dare ask who or what happened to you?"

"The church fell on me."

"Literally or figuratively?"

"Both, I think."

"Then you're lucky to be alive." Martin waved the note

paper in his hand, being careful to miss the bottle of amber liquid on the desk in front of him. "I was just about to leave you the bad news, chapter and verse on survival in Mormon Country."

Traveler stretched out on the floor and began doing limbering exercises. "I'll take it lying down, if you don't mind."

"Not funny." Martin crushed the note paper into a ball and threw it at his son. Then he raised the bottle and drank.

"What the hell is that?" Traveler asked.

"Something Doc Murphy prescribed."

"It looks like scotch."

"It's a better painkiller than that, believe me. You look like you need a shot yourself."

Martin screwed on the cap and came around the desk to hand it to his son. The bottle had a warning label that said this drug may cause drowsiness, that its effect may be intensified with alcohol, and that care should be used when operating a car or dangerous machinery. The dosage was two tablespoons every two hours, not to exceed twelve tablespoons in any twenty-four hour period.

"How much have you had so far?" Traveler asked.

"That's my business. Besides, I've got another bottle if I need it. Now quit stalling and tell me what happened."

Traveler groaned and handed back the bottle. "Two guys came after me in the parking lot."

"Only two. From the way you limped in here I figured a ward of deacons must have jumped you. Did you recognize them?"

"They didn't look LDS, if that's what you mean."

Martin sighed with relief. "Maybe they weren't church at all."

"I wouldn't bet on it."

"Look, son, I made the calls you wanted. At first I couldn't get anything concrete. Just hints and innuendo that I was on dangerous ground. Finally a friend at Immigration and Naturalization came right out and told me, *and you*, to lay off Maria Gomez. She's federal jurisdiction. No private eyes allowed."

"That's bullshit and you know it. She's a witness in a murder case. That's strictly local."

"Local or federal doesn't cut it in this state. I know that. You know that. The only thing that counts here is church jurisdiction."

Traveler grunted and kept on stretching his leg.

"Listen to me," his father continued. "Messing around with Willis Tanner is one thing. He's a friend, as much as can be with a gentile like you."

Traveler stopped exercising and sat up. Was it a slip of the tongue, or had Martin purposely left himself out of the cast of gentiles present?

Martin coughed and took another swallow from the bottle, which was already half empty. "But Miles Beecham is another matter altogether. He just got off the phone with me. If you weren't my son, you'd be in jail right now."

"Those were his boys who came after me."

"Are you sure?"

"I'm not sure of anything."

Martin sighed. "Miles wouldn't do something like that unless it was for your own good."

"Do you trust him?"

Martin thought that over for a moment. "On this, I do. So far you haven't done anything to hurt the church. But if dogma ever gets in the way, Miles won't have any choice. You can't blame a man for being true to his beliefs."

"Murder has nothing to do with God."

Martin looked shocked. "You can't actually believe the church is involved."

Traveler lay back and went through thirty seconds of deep-breathing exercises before answering. "Not officially. But something's going on. Whether Willis is involved or your buddy Miles, I don't know. One thing's for sure. Somebody with power is playing games."

"If that's the case, I have a solution. We'll spend a day or two in Kamas. With luck the dust will have settled by the time we get back. We can also get out of this goddamned heat."

Traveler stood up and tested his leg. The cramp was gone, the pain wasn't. He limped back and forth across the narrow office. When he came to a stop in front of the open window, he leaned against the sill and peered out at the temple. A siren sounded in the distance, giving the impression that the golden statue of Moroni had raised his trumpet to call the faithful to prayer.

Traveler said a silent prayer of his own.

Martin laid a hand on his son's shoulder. "I hope you can understand what I'm going through."

"I'll come with you to Kamas, Dad."

"I'm not so sick I can't drive myself."

"I've got to stop in Provo anyway."

"It's out of the way."

"On a day like this it will be a nice drive."

Martin grabbed him from behind and hugged. The embrace, which would have embarrassed them face to face, went on until the phone rang.

"Moroni Traveler and Son," Martin answered. His voice, taut with emotion, was barely audible.

Traveler turned around in time to see his father mouth silently, "It's Claire."

Traveler clenched the receiver so hard he half expected her voice to sound strangled. Instead, she was buoyant. "I'm saved at last. The Angel Moroni has answered my call."

"I was on my way out," he said, his voice cold despite the heat she evoked inside.

"You know the rules," she said.

He waited.

"You're supposed to ask where I am."

"But I know the answer already."

"I'm lost," she said.

"I can't find you, Claire. I never could."

"You're a detective. It's your job to find people."

He'd gone after her before. The last time he'd nearly killed someone.

He heard laughter in the background. If she was following her usual pattern, she was calling from a bar. When the sound increased he knew she was holding the receiver away from her ear. As if on cue someone sang, "Angel Mary heist your leg, take that Mormon down a peg, while I roll your sister Meg upon the parlor floor."

Claire came back on the line to say "That's a clue, Moroni."

She used to croon the same verse to him when they were making love.

"Come find me," she said, switching to her little girl's voice.

"Your apartment is on Second Avenue between A and B Streets."

"You've been keeping track of me." She sounded delighted. "But I'm not home now, so that means I'm still lost."

"I have work to do," he said.

"Have you forgotten the first time you found me? The reward I gave you."

A half breath, half moan came down the line, the kind of sound she made at the approach of orgasm. When he failed to respond, her gasp grew louder. Was she performing for him, he wondered, or those in the bar?

He had given up his apartment and moved in with Claire a week after meeting her. She was unlike the other women he'd been attracted to, thin, hardly any breasts to speak of, with a fragile quality that made him feel protective.

"Put your hands around me," she'd say as they undressed, directing his hands so that his fingers completely encircled her waist. "You could squeeze me to death if you wanted to."

"I love you."

"But you could, couldn't you?"

Within weeks she'd gained enough weight so that his hands no longer reached. She did so without ever seeming to eat.

"It's you I feed upon," she had told him.

Over the phone her gasping climax sounded in his ear, too real for the best of actresses.

"Good-bye, Claire."

"I know you, Moroni. You'll have to find me to say good-bye."

17

Traveler drove down State Street, the old Highway 89, instead of using the freeway. Haze from the smelters to the west had taken enough bite out of the three o'clock sun to make the ride comfortable. But the air, coming in through the Jeep's open windows, smelled as if it had been breathed too many times before.

When Traveler turned east on Thirty-third South, Martin's snort of disapproval turned into a cough. He took a swig of medicine and gargled noisily before swallowing.

"Goddamn. That's got a kick. But I'm still sober enough to know you're going the wrong way."

"I thought we should talk to the Farnsworth girl before leaving town."

"I don't remember being consulted."

"They live in The Cove. We can pick up the Bonneville Freeway from there."

Martin sucked a breath as if preparing to argue. But a fit of coughing doubled him over. Half a minute went by before he calmed enough to swallow another mouthful of medicine.

Traveler pulled over to the side of the road and stopped. "I think I'd better take you home, Dad."

Martin's answer was to make a show of sniffing fumes from the open bottle. "Here I am, a sick old man on my way to be cured by faith healers and you're making detours."

Traveler forced a smile. For the first time all day Martin sounded like himself.

"Are you drunk?"

Martin held a cupped palm in front of his face and blew into it, as if trying to smell his breath.

"Here," Traveler said, handing over a package of spearmint gum.

With a grin, Martin fed a stick into his mouth and began chewing elaborately. After a moment he breathed into his palm again. "There's nothing like the smell of a Jack Mormon."

"You've never been a member of the church in good standing, so you don't qualify."

"Are you sure of that?"

"Don't go maudlin on me and start confessing the sins of your youth."

"That's no way to speak about your mother."

"You'd better give me that medicine for safe-keeping."

"You drive, I'll drink," Martin said, but screwed the cap on just the same and slipped the bottle into the glove compartment.

Once Traveler was back on the road, his father said, "Claire is a lot like your mother was, you know."

Traveler took his eyes from Thirty-third South long enough to check his father's expression. But Martin was leaning back against the headrest with his eyes closed.

"They were both lost to us right from the beginning."

Traveler stared straight ahead.

"Kary was so beautiful." Martin seldom referred to his wife, Traveler's mother, as Kary. "Like Claire, she could stop a man's heart."

They were passing Twenty-seventh East, heading up into the foothills of the Wasatch Mountains. Though the temperature was still in the high eighties, the gray granite peaks, Brigham Young's barrier against his eastern enemies, looked cold and uninviting.

"Unfortunately, it wasn't my heart she was interested in," Martin said, stretching until his hands touched the windshield.

"I know the feeling."

"I've never given you advice about women before, have I?"

"Not in so many words."

Martin chuckled. "Don't worry. I'm not about to start now. Still, speaking as a detective, have you ever thought of hiring one of our colleagues to keep an eye on Claire? That way, the next time she calls you'll be one up on her."

"She goes a month between calls sometimes. I couldn't have her followed that long."

"Kary taught me enough about women to know that Claire's not going to wait that long, not after today's performance. You can take my word for it."

"Rest your throat, Dad."

"If a son's going to tell his father to shut up, that's as nice a way as any to do it." Martin settled back in his seat and pretended to snore.

Traveler turned right on Wasatch Boulevard and then left on Millcreek. The community known as The Cove was nestled at the base of Mount Olympus, part of the western face of the Wasatch Mountains. They were well over a mile high at this point, more than a thousand feet above the valley floor, and the air was a good five degrees cooler than downtown.

The Farnsworth house had attempted a modern style but concessions to Utah's winters had destroyed the effect. Too much gray brick and concrete had seen to that.

Traveler, with Martin at his side, rang the bell. A moment later the drapes on a front window parted and Suzanne Farnsworth peered out. Her face, which showed no signs of recognition, disappeared when Traveler smiled.

Nothing happened for nearly a minute. Traveler was

about to ring again when the inner door opened. The screen door, of heavy aluminum that would convert to a glass storm door in winter, remained in place.

"My father's at work and my mother's at the store," she said.

"This is my father, Suzanne. We'd like to talk to you."

"My father doesn't want me letting people in when I'm here alone."

"We can talk out here if you'd like."

Traveler and Martin backed away from the door so she wouldn't feel threatened. She joined them on the concrete slab that served as a walkway.

"I need to know more about your fiancé," Traveler said.

"Like what?"

"You told me that he called himself a missionary of the damned in his last letter."

She nodded.

"Did he often write things like that?"

"Of course not."

"What would make him do such a thing?"

Next door a neighbor came out and started watering, an obvious ruse to eavesdrop.

"You'd better come inside," Suzanne said.

She held the door for Traveler and his father, leaving it unlocked as if to make escape easier if need be, and then ushered them into a living room that smelled faintly of chocolate. The room itself was large, a good twenty by thirty feet, with light-brown wall-to-wall carpet, over which clear plastic runners had been laid creating paths to other rooms. The furniture looked brand-new and gave the impression of having been selected from black-and-white catalog photographs, with a resulting mix of colors that clashed violently. The white plaster walls were uncluttered by paintings or other decorations.

Traveler and Martin sat on a maroon davenport facing a feather-rock fireplace in which nothing had ever been burned. Directly in front of them a glass-topped coffee table held carefully arranged magazines, *The New Era* and *Improvement Era*, both church publications. Suzanne settled into an adjacent chair, matching the sofa in style but whose color reminded Traveler of a soda fountain drink of his childhood known as a Green River.

"You were about to tell me why your fiancé might call himself a missionary of the damned."

"But I don't know."

"Was it a religious statement on his part?"

"We're both members of the church. We didn't need to talk about it."

Martin spoke for the first time, his voice hoarse. "Young men about to go on missions usually talk about their work."

Suzanne blushed and looked away. "We were in love. When we were alone we necked. I wanted to get married right away, but Heber said the mission came first. He could quote Joseph Smith by heart, you know. He made me learn it, too."

She paused. Her head tilted to one side as if she were listening to something beyond their hearing. "'Go in all meekness, in sobriety, and preach Jesus Christ and Him crucified; not to contend with others on account of their faith, or systems of religion, but pursue a steady course. This I delivered by way of commandment, and all who observe it not, will pull down persecution upon their heads, while those who do, shall always be filled with the Holy Ghost; this I pronounced as a prophecy.'"

Suzanne ducked her head as if embarrassed by her performance, then reached beneath her chair and brought out a box of chocolate-covered cherries. She popped one into her mouth before absently offering the box to Martin and Traveler. Both declined.

"He sounds like a religious young man," Martin said.

"Heber's parents expected it of him. So did my father." She fed another chocolate into her mouth.

Traveler picked up a copy of *Improvement Era*. The mailing label was addressed to Bishop Newell Farnsworth. "Has your father ever tried other religions?"

She swallowed abruptly. "Is that some kind of trick question?"

"He introduced us to a man called Orson Pack and made certain we all shook hands."

"Uncle Orson, you mean. . . ."

Both Traveler and his father nodded.

"We're on our way to see him," Martin clarified. "At least I am."

Suzanne put her chocolates down on the coffee table and stared at him intently for a moment. "He's really my father's uncle, but I call him Uncle just the same. He's been spending the holidays with us as long as I can remember. Every Thanksgiving he brings pies he makes himself from home-grown pumpkins. Heber met him here on Thanksgiving two years ago. They talked for hours."

"What about?" Traveler asked.

She blushed again. "I didn't hear all of it. I was helping Mom with the food and washing dishes most of the time. But they talked about God a lot. Once, when they didn't know I could hear them, I heard them discussing sex. Uncle Orson wanted Heber to think about what he was doing."

"In what way?"

"He knew Heber and I were lusting after each other."

"There's nothing wrong with that," Martin said.

"Uncle Orson doesn't believe in sex or children."

18

The city of Provo, thirty-five miles south of Salt Lake, is the home of Brigham Young University. It was also the birthplace of Traveler's father who, once they were inside the city limits, insisted that they pull over to the side of the road and listen for meadowlarks. Their song, he'd been saying ever since Traveler could remember, sang the praise of his hometown.

Martin whistled a meadowlark's tune and then, as always, sang the words he said went with it. "Provo is a pretty little place."

There was no answer to his call. The only birds in the neighborhood were sparrows, and they weren't singing.

"This all used to be open fields," Martin said, staring up at Mount Timpanogos, an 11,750-foot peak in the Wasatch Front that overshadowed Provo. "I remember hiking on the glacier up there as a kid. There was nothing like it. The air was crisp and clear. It was like that down here, too. I could smell the mountain pines every day when I was walking to school."

Martin searched for his youth with a deep breath. What he found sent him back to the car for a swallow of cough medicine.

"That was before the steel plant got built," he explained when he came up for air.

Traveler grunted and starting driving again. Their destination, the Missionary Training Center, was, like most Mormon architecture, plain and functional. So were the young men in evidence. They all had short hair and wore two-piece suits with white shirts and ties.

"It reminds me of the army," Martin said. "You go ahead and take care of your business. I'm going to walk around for a while."

"Listening for meadowlarks?"

"You never know."

Traveler watched until Martin turned the corner and disappeared from sight. His chances of finding meadowlarks were about as good as Traveler getting what he wanted out of the bureaucracy inside.

The only security in evidence was a waist-high counter. Behind it were several desks, each with its own computer terminal and operator typing in information, and a middle-aged man whose face looked too innocent to be anything but a bishop in the making.

"I'm Elder Dixon," he said. "May I help you?"

"I have a nephew who's overseas on a mission. I haven't seen him in years and wanted to find out how he's doing. Or if he needs anything."

"Are you talking about a donation?"

"I have my checkbook with me."

"What is your name, sir?"

"Martin Armstrong," Traveler improvised. "My nephew is Heber Armstrong, named after the church president and prophet."

"Do you understand how we work?"

"It's been a long time," Traveler said, as if implying that he had once been on a mission himself.

"Here at the center we've taken a page from the military. We look upon this as boot camp for God's recruits. Our missionaries are cut off from the secular worries of the outside world. Their only concern is to work hard in the name of the Lord. After all, we have very little time to get them ready for foreign service."

"It must be difficult teaching language and custom."

The elder's nostrils flared as if he'd caught the scent of sin, like cigarette smoke, clinging to Traveler.

"Our studies here concentrate on memorizing appropriate areas of *The Book of Mormon*. Surely you know that. The techniques of door-to-door salesmanship must be taught. You can't count on people to recognize the truth without a fight."

Traveler hoped a nod would suffice.

"Each of our missionaries is endowed with the Holy Priesthood and is sent forth as a minister of the restored Gospel of our Lord and Savior. Now, what was the name of your nephew again?"

"Heber Armstrong."

Elder Dixon relayed the name to one of the young men, who immediately began typing information into his computer terminal.

While they were waiting for the information to be processed, the phone rang. The other young man in the office answered. "It's for you, sir," he said to Dixon.

He squinted at Traveler before turning away to pick up the receiver. A moment later he swung back to look Traveler up and down. "He's about six feet four inches tall, maybe two hundred and thirty pounds. Dark hair. Blue eyes. Strange blue eyes."

The elder stopped speaking and began to nod. When he hung up the phone a few moments later, his hands were shaking. "Are you going to leave or should I call the police?"

Traveler handed the man a business card and quoted *The Book of Mormon* on his way out. " 'Yea, verily, verily I say unto you, if all men had been, and were, and ever would be, like unto Moroni, behold, the very powers of hell would have been shaken forever.' "

Martin was waiting in the car.

"Did you hear any meadowlarks?" Traveler asked.

Martin whistled as if checking pitch, then sang, "Provo is a pretty little place."

Traveler shook his head. "We'd better get going. I don't want to hit the High Uintas in the dark."

19

Their route took them northeast on Highway 89, a steady climb into the Uinta Mountains. When they'd left Provo at five in the afternoon the temperature had been eighty-four degrees. By the time they reached Kamas at the edge of the High Uinta Primitive Area two hours later, the Jeep's heater was having a hard time keeping them warm.

They filled the gas tank at the Chevron station and asked direction to the Saints of the Last Day.

The attendant, a weatherbeaten man wearing a blue baseball cap with BYU lettered in white on the front, gave Traveler a funny look and shrugged. "Only thing I know for sure is that we're getting snow tonight."

"In July?"

"When you've lived in these mountains as long as I have, mister, you'll know better than to count on it being summertime."

"If you've been here so long, you ought to know where we can find the Saints."

He scratched one of his dark, shaggy sideburns. "If you was LDS, you'd know a Saint when you saw one."

Martin stepped in front of Traveler and said, "I'm on my way to meet with Brother Orson Pack. Maybe you've heard of him."

The attendant took off his cap, exposing his shiny bald head. "You looking for a cure?"

"What I'm looking for is information."

"You might try the café," the man said, running a hand over his head before pointing down Kamas's main street. "You can't miss it. All the sinners eat there sooner or later."

THE KAMAS CAFÉ was written in blue neon. Coors Beer blinked in red. Cigarette smoke mixed with the smell of hamburgers and French fries billowed out when Traveler opened the door.

Inside there was standing-room only and enough noise to make conversation impossible at anything but a shout. Men and women were lined two deep along a bar that ran the length of the building, which was knotty pine from floor to ceiling. Judging by the looks of the rough-hewn wood, the café went back to the days when Kamas had been carved out of the surrounding forest. The same wood had been used to build booths along the two walls on either side of the bar. Tables lined the other wall. One of them, the table nearest the jukebox, had two people—a man and woman dressed in cowboy hats, jeans, and boots—and four chairs. Martin went over to them and bent over the table until his head was only inches from theirs. After a moment, he glanced back at his son and waved at him to join them.

"Meet the Hansons," Martin bellowed as soon as Traveler sat down. "Gwen and Lester. They've invited us to share their table."

Both had the bloated look of beer drinkers, with red, fleshy faces as bright as the Coors neon outside.

The woman, somewhere in her forties, leaned so close Traveler could taste her perfume. "Your father tells us you're a professional football player."

Beneath the table Travler clenched his fists. His father knew how much he hated playing the good old boy in bars, slapping backs and trading memories. They inevitably led to pain, and sometimes violence.

"That was a long time ago," he said through his teeth.

His father smiled apologetically, pointed to his mouth, and chewed up and down to show he was hungry.

A sudden lull in noise level made conversation possible at someting less than a holler.

"Goddamn," Lester said. "I remember you now. One crazy fucker on Monday Night Football. Named after an angel, someone said once. But you played like the devil."

Gwen's eyes brightened. "You still look good enough to play." Her long red nails, nearly an inch beyond her fingertips, clacked on the tabletop.

"Crippled some poor bastard, didn't you?" Lester went on.

"Is there a waitress?" Martin asked. "Or do you have to get your own food around here?"

"I'll put in a word for you," Lester volunteered. "What would you like to eat?"

"What's good?"

"Nothing. But everybody comes here for the burgers anyway."

"Two burgers it is then. And two beers."

"Better not," Traveler said.

"Mo's right. We've got to see a man."

"Who are you looking for?" Gwen asked once her husband had left to put in the order. One hand began walking its way across the table toward Traveler.

"The Saints of the Last Day."

Her fingers, like participants in some child's game, backed up. "Shit. A big hunk like you. I should have known it was too good to be true in a town like Kamas. All we ever get around here besides Mormons is misfits."

Crablike, her hand moved back and forth on the table while her eyes, surrounded in blue makeup, watched Traveler.

"It ain't natural," she said, "men living out there together like that. They can't kid me. All the goody-two-shoes talk. Bullshit, I say. I don't care what they call themselves. Something's going on. It has to be."

"Where are we talking about?" Traveler asked.

One finger raised up, waving in his direction like an insect's antennae. "Are you here to join up and call yourself a saint?"

"Do I look like a saint?"

Her hand turned over on its back. The antennae became a beckoning finger. "Come home with me. I'll show you how to find God."

Martin started to cough. Traveler couldn't tell if it was the cigarette smoke or his father's way of putting an end to the conversation.

"I'll get you something to drink," Traveler said, and started to stand up.

"You'd better make the burgers to go," Martin managed to say.

Gwen smiled as if she thought Martin intended to take the food home with her.

"I'll be right back," Traveler said, and headed for the bar, where Lester had yet to order.

Traveler held out a twenty-dollar bill to the sweating bartender. "Two burgers and two coffees to go and no change."

Five minutes later he returned to the table with a brown bag in hand and directions to the Saints of the Last Day in his head.

Gwen stood up to meet him. "Come on, you two. Lester's good here for hours."

"So are you," Martin said, and sat her back down.

Traveler fed money into the jukebox and soon Johnny Cash was drowning out her protests.

20

State Highway 150 climbs to 11,000 feet before making its way across the Uinta Mountains into Wyoming. At Mirror Lake, elevation 10,500 feet, it was snowing when Traveler parked in front of a long-dead lodge that was serving as headquarters for the Saints of the Last Day. Night had just snuffed out the last dregs of light.

They were met by a man carrying a kerosene lantern that hissed like a night insect. He was dressed in black trousers and a black broadcloth coat buttoned to the neck. His face looked dead white in the artificial light.

"Welcome. I'm Brother Moab, first disciple to Brother Orson. He thought we'd be having guests sometime soon." Brother Moab raised the lantern to spread its light and beckoned them to follow in his footsteps. "Be careful. It's already getting slippery."

They passed several small cabins, leaking light from windows and cracked walls alike, on their way to what had once been the lodge's dining room. Half a dozen lanterns provided a steady hiss of background static, while exposing a long, narrow room with a vaulted ceiling. It reminded Traveler of a church. It had no furniture, only a line of logs that served as makeshift pews, on which sat fifteen or twenty men dressed in black trousers and white home-spun shirts. All wore straggly beards that made them look like Orthodox Jews. One was young, the rest gray-haired.

Orson Pack stood at the head of the room, silhouetted against a roaring fire, and beckoned them with open arms. "As the good book says, 'I will visit and soften their hearts, many of them for your good, that ye may find grace in their eyes, that they may come to the light of truth, and the Gentiles to the exaltation or lifting up of Zion.'"

When he finished speaking his followers rose and chorused, "Amen." Their trousers, Traveler noticed, buttoned in the back.

The room smelled of smoke and the sour sweat of old men. Gusts of cold air whistled through chinks in the walls, causing the firelight to cast wild, flickering shadows. As a result, the men's faces seemed to writhe with a life of their own.

"Come forward, Martin Traveler," Pack said. "Sit here before us." He indicated the wooden floor at the head of the pews.

Martin cast a quick look at his son before moving to the front of the room, where he eased himself into a cross-legged position on the worn planks. The constantly shifting patterns of light made his face indistinguishable from those nearest him.

Brother Moab nudged Traveler gently from behind. The detective allowed himself to be herded forward until he was seated on the first pew. Pack came over to stand beside him. His hand reached out, hovering over Traveler's head.

He spoke to his followers. "This is the man I told you about. Moroni, Martin's son."

Pack's touch was charged with static electricity. "We understand your cynicism, Moroni. It has gnawed upon us all at one time or another. I see it in your eyes. You're angry because your father has turned to us at a time like this. But if you look deeply into yourself, you'll see a glimpse of your own future in your father's actions. He is a preview of what happens to us all, believer and nonbeliever alike, when mortality catches up with us. Don't hold that against him or us. Are we less because we turn to God in the face of death?"

Pack removed his hand and knelt before Traveler. "God himself sought out His prophet, Joseph Smith, in Kirkland, Ohio, in 1831 to deliver His answer. 'For the day cometh that the Lord shall utter His voice out of heaven; the heavens shall shake and the earth shall tremble, and the trump of God shall sound both long and loud, and shall say to the sleeping nations: Ye saints arise and live; ye sinners stay and sleep until I shall call again.'"

Traveler stared into the man's eyes. Despite reflections of firelight, he saw nothing there to fear, and much to envy. Pack smiled before gesturing to his flock. Half a dozen of the oldest men came forward. They circled Martin and bowed their heads, their bodies swaying from side to side in time with a music only they could hear.

After a moment Pack rose to his feet and joined their circle. When he spoke again it was to Martin. "We ask you to understand us. Our search for God has turned us away from all but the true prophets, Joseph Smith and Brigham Young. Those who followed in their footsteps were false prophets. They preached change, change for the sake of convenience and greed. There is no profit in the status quo, they would tell us. So let us have change. Isn't it inevitable anyway?"

Pack stopped speaking to stare at those nearest him. "I ask you, what good has change done us? Look around. People are drowning in immorality."

Traveler groaned inwardly. He'd heard that lament before, from men grown too old to remember clearly the impatience of their youth. Judging from the look on his father's face, Martin also recognized such sour grapes. Yet there was no denying Pack's sincerity. A con man wouldn't have hidden himself away in the High Uintas.

Pack half turned to point out the buttons at the back of his trousers. "The fly in the front came into fashion for only one reason, to create fornication pants, as Brigham Young called them. 'They're an invention of the devil,' he told us. 'They make things too easy; it's a temptation, and takes your mind off your work. I heard of a case in San

Francisco where a man's hardly had his buttoned up since he got them. If I can help it, the Latter-day Saints of the Church of Jesus Christ will wear pants that open on the sides; they're plenty good enough, and speedy enough, for us in Salt Lake City. And I hope the women don't encourage things to the contrary.'"

After patting his own behind, Pack continued. "Brigham said, 'My pantaloons button up here where they belong, that my secrets, that God has given me, should not be exposed.' But we here assembled have gone the prophet one better. We've removed temptation from the side to the back."

He stopped speaking to walk among his followers. When he'd completed his tour he came back to sit beside Traveler.

"Brigham tried to help women walk the moral path. He designed chaste garments for them, which he called his *Deseret Costume.* But the women, even some of his own wives, insisted on following the fashions set by gentiles. And our prophet said, 'The women say, let us wear hoops, because the whores wear them. I believe if they were to come with a cob stuck in their behind, you would want to do the same. I despise their damnable fashions, their lying and whoring; and God being my helper, I'll live to see every one of those cussed fools off the earth, saint or sinner. Who cares about these infernal gentiles? If they wear a piss pot on their head, must I do so?'"

Pack paused, whether for breath or to eye Traveler for the gentile he was, the detective didn't know.

"Do you wonder that the Saints of the Last Day have forsaken women altogether? Our name should tell you the answer. The world ends on the last day. We here hasten its approach by refusing to produce offspring."

He walked among his followers once again, laying his hands upon them one after the other. Finally he stopped before the youngest of his flock, whose beard was still dark and luxuriant. "I call upon you, my brother, to share your strength of youth with Martin."

The man couldn't have been more than thirty, which prompted Traveler to wonder what kind of faith would drive a man in his prime to hide himself away in the mountains with old men. Perhaps the same kind of passion that demanded celibacy of Catholic priests. Or maybe it was madness, Traveler decided after catching a glimpse of the young man's eyes. The madness of a zealot.

The Saints, even those who'd been circling Martin, formed a double line so that the young man could walk between them, receiving the touch of each as he passed by. He sighed as each hand fell upon him. His eyes widened and flashed, growing brighter by the touch, as if he was storing the combined power of their contact within him.

When finally all had laid hands upon him, he turned to look at Orson Pack, who was now at Traveler's side. Pack nodded and the young man leapt forward to take Martin's head between his hands.

Martin cried out.

"The evil is being driven from him," Pack said, restraining Traveler.

Martin writhed for a moment, then grew quiet.

"Come," said Pack, leading Traveler to his father. "All here must now lay hands upon Brother Martin."

Some knelt, some crouched, others stood so that all could touch Martin at the same time. When every hand was in place, Pack raised his head toward the heavens. "Lord, give us the power to heal your servant. Fill him, and all of us, with your goodness. Lord, we . . ." He faltered. His eyes widened as he stared from face to face.

"Amen," someone picked up.

The others joined in as one.

Traveler's *amen* was to himself.

Pack removed his hands. The others followed his example.

"From the book," he said. "'And it supposeth me that they have come hither to hear the pleasing word of God, yea, the word which healeth the wounded soul.'"

With that Orson Pack reached out to Martin, took him

by the hands, and helped him to his feet. "You and your son must leave us now. I will show you the way."

He took a lantern from a wall peg and led them outside, where a quarter moon was lighting a sky full of stars. Their breaths billowed in the clear air. A thin layer of frozen snow crackled underfoot.

"We can thank God that storms pass quickly in these mountains. Otherwise you'd have to stay the night."

Through the trees, Traveler caught a glimpse of moonlight reflecting off the icy road. "That might be best."

"You must go quickly."

"Why?" Martin asked, blinking in the lantern light. He was hugging himself against the cold, all the more intense because of the warmth they'd left behind.

Pack caught his breath. "Surely you felt it when all our hands came together?"

Martin blinked uncertainly.

"I'm not talking about the touch of God." Pack set the lantern in the snow at his feet and took hold of first Martin's hand and then Traveler's. He peered anxiously into their faces for a long time. Finally he nodded as if reassured by what he saw.

"There was no healing here tonight," he told them. "Evil has come among us."

"I don't understand," Traveler said, but Pack had already scooped up the lantern and was hurrying toward the Jeep.

When they caught up with him he was shaking. Through chattering teeth he said, "I have sought the Devil's touch all my life. And now that I've felt it I'm afraid. My faith may not be strong enough to cleanse even my own sins."

Martin opened his mouth to say something but starting coughing instead.

"I'm sorry," Pack said. "I did my best."

"Get in," Traveler told him, opening the Jeep's door. "There's more to be said."

After a instant's hesitation Pack climbed into the back. Traveler helped his father into the passenger's seat, and then slid behind the wheel himself and started the engine so the heater could go to work.

Martin retrieved his cough medicine from the glove compartment and upended the bottle. His swallows were so noisy Traveler could count the mouthfuls. After three of them his father came up for air, breathing carefully to test his throat. When he didn't cough, he sighed and settled back against the bucket seat.

Traveler switched on the interior light so he could watch Pack in the rearview mirror. "When Newell Farnsworth introduced us outside the police building, why didn't you say you were a relative of the family?" he asked Pack.

"I thought that was obvious."

"We need to know more about Heber if we're to have any chance of finding him."

"He's like a son to me," Pack said.

"But the Saints of the Last Day don't believe in offspring."

"Ours is a hard road, I admit that. Sometimes we stray."

"The Farnsworth girl says you tried to talk him out of marrying her."

Something showed in Pack's face. It might have been embarrassment. "He was young. The heat within him was too great to join the Saints at that time."

Traveler swung around to see if the mirror had missed anything. At their first meeting Orson Pack had seemed a man perfectly composed. But now his eyes were restive, as if they'd seen more than was good for them.

"When was the last time you saw Heber Armstrong?" Traveler asked.

"The boy I knew was lost to me when he left for his mission. Now, if you'll excuse me, I must get back. The evil one must be driven from our midst."

"I hope you have more luck with him than you did with my father's illness."

Pack stared down at the folded hands in his lap. "I deserve your scorn. Because of me, your belief is stillborn."

"And my father?"

"I've heard about a woman near here who does pioneer cures. Go back down the highway about a mile, just beyond the range cattle sign. There's a dirt road leading off to the right. You can't miss it. Emma Kimball's shack is about a hundred yards farther on. You can walk it from here if you prefer. In daylight there's a path to follow."

"Is she to be our second opinion?" Traveler asked.

Pack's hands squeezed together; his fingers writhed. "There are people in Kamas who swear by her."

"And the Saints? Do they make use of her services despite their rejection of women?"

Martin's elbow dug into Traveler's side.

Traveler reached across the seat and opened the back door. Pack got out without another word.

21

Caught in the flashlight's beam, Emma Kimball looked as old and moth-eaten as an Egyptian mummy whose wrappings had come loose. One glimpse of her and Traveler felt foolish for suspecting hanky-panky with the Saints of the Last Day.

For lack of anything better he said, "Orson Pack sent us."

She smiled, exposing teeth the color of old ivory. Her eyes remained hidden under heavy, sagging lids. Her neck, protruding from gray, one-piece overalls, looked as fragile as a twig. "This late at night I was hoping for more excitement than that."

"I'm surprised you opened the door."

"I'm a hundred years old, fer chrissake." She touched her cheek, a girlish gesture meant to deny the statement. But her fingers came away suddenly, as if they'd found something they didn't like. "There's nothing here to steal, including my virtue."

She shuffled back out of the way, an invitation to come inside. Travler sidestepped, deferring to his father, who'd insisted on diverting the Jeep down a road so badly rutted only the four-wheel drive had saved them.

"Which one of you's sick?" she asked as soon as they were inside.

"I am," Martin said.

The atmosphere inside the cabin was as thick as fog, its smell so astringent Traveler's sinuses started throbbing. The room was no more than twenty feet square and lighted by an old-fashioned kerosene lamp smoking so badly its glass chimney had turned black. A narrow bed stood against one wall, beneath the room's only window. Most of the remaining floor space, except for a well-worn path leading to the bed, was taken up by tables of varying sizes and shapes, including a picnic table with attached benches. Pots, pans, tin cans, and buckets were strewn everywhere, stirring ladles protruding from a few of them.

Emma leaned toward Martin and touched a gnarled finger to the side of her nose. "Have you been drinking?"

Sheepishly he fished the medicine bottle from his back pocket and showed it to her.

Her eyes opened wide enough to show pleasure. "That would never get past the Word of Wisdom."

Jesus, Traveler thought. Here they were in the wilds of Utah, visiting a woman who would have been called a witch a hundred years ago, and there was still no escaping Joseph Smith's revelation outlawing liquor and tobacco. The whole thing was inspired, some say, because the prophet's first wife got tired of Joe and his cronies carousing in her house and spitting tobacco juice on her floor.

"Let me see that." Emma took the bottle away from Martin and held it under her nose.

Maybe witch was the right name for her, no matter what the century. Judging by the numb feeling in Traveler's nose, it would take black magic to sort one smell from another in such a sated atmosphere.

"Doctors tried to kill me off ninety years ago," Emma said. "That's when my mother started teaching me how to cure. She lived to be nearly a hundred herself. By then I was ministering to her. She never suffered, I can tell you that."

With a look of disgust she handed the bottle back to

Martin. "You keep drinking this and the doctors will do you in too. Look at you, fer chrissake. You look like an old man. A man your age should still be voting for polygamy."

Martin rubbed his throat. "The doctors say I have a tumor."

"They can say whatever they want. Emma believes only her eyes."

She led Martin to the picnic table, cleared enough bench space for him to sit, and then fetched the lamp from the stand next to her bed. As soon as she turned up the wick, she reached into an overall pocket and extracted wire-rimmed spectacles, which she adjusted halfway down her nose.

"Open wide," she said, "and say ah."

Her hands and nails, Traveler noticed, looked freshly scrubbed. Watching her peer and probe made him nervous, so he moved cautiously around the table, checking the pots and pans as he went. The mixtures they contained varied from liquids, both thick and thin, to dried grasses. His nose still had enough life to catch a few variations in smell, though the overall impact was something approaching menthol.

One container held a syrup so thick a ladle had been trapped standing straight up. He pulled it free of the mess and brought it within range of his nose. His throat spasmed, causing him to gag.

"Don't go mocking things you don't understand," the old woman said.

By the time he'd replaced the ladle, she was unbuttoning Martin's shirt and pressing her ear against his chest.

"Breathe deeply, old man."

"Damn it," Martin said. "I'm a hell of a lot younger than you are."

Emma cackled. "My last husband had ten years on you and he could do it every night."

"What happened to him?"

She nudged Martin suggestively. "I wore him out."

Martin nudged back. "I thought you could heal anything."

"You youngsters. He was just like you. Thought he knew everything. Shoot. If he'd listened to me he'd still be warming my bed."

She fingered a small cloth bag that was hanging around her neck. "You see this? I've worn one every day of my life since I was sick as a girl. Lew, that's my husband, wouldn't wear his to bed. Said he didn't like the smell. You can't tell some people what's good for them. They're the same kind who say there's no cure for the common cold, but don't you believe it. Why, right now there's a summer virus going around down in Kamas."

She squeezed the bag gently. "Many a person's been carried away by a summer cold, Lew included. That's why you won't see me taking any chances. An asafetida bag is the only sure way. My mother knew that and she came across with Brigham Young back in forty-seven. It cured then, it cures now."

She left Martin's side to rummage in one of the nightstand's drawers. After a moment she came up with another small cloth bag attached to a rawhide loop, a twin of the one around her own neck. With the bag in hand she moved back to the picnic table and scooped a handful of dark material from one of the bowls.

"Asafetida." She held out her packed fist. "Take a whiff of that. It sure beats store-bought."

Both father and son obliged. It reminded Traveler of garlic, though he couldn't be sure because of the condition of his nose.

Emma made a clucking noise as she stuffed the bag, cinching its drawstring and knotting it tightly around the rawhide. That done, she spread the leather loop and signaled Martin to bow his head. Once the bag was around his neck, she stepped back and nodded with satisfaction.

"As long as I've been curing sore throats, asafetida's never failed me yet."

"And tumors?" Traveler asked.

She sighed. "I don't know."

"I'd hate to have to go through life smelling like this for nothing," Martin said.

"You come back one of these days and maybe I'll let you into my bed after all."

Traveler took hold of his father. "Come on. We've got a long drive in the dark."

Emma wrapped a shawl around her shoulders and followed them to the door. "If it gets worse you can always try tying a dirty sock around your neck. An onion on a string's good, too, or a piece of unwashed lamb's hair that's been soaked in brandy."

The night air started Martin coughing.

"Hold the bag to your nose and breathe deeply," Emma advised.

As soon as Martin did, the coughing subsided.

"Thank you," Traveler said as he helped his father into the Jeep.

"I've tried all the cures," she called after them. "I still say asafetida's the best."

22

Martin didn't want to spend the night in a Kamas motel, so Traveler drove straight through to Salt Lake, fighting mountain roads and exhaustion until he reached home at two in the morning. Even at that hour the temperature, according to the car radio, was seventy-seven degrees.

Traveler recognized Claire's perfume as soon as he stepped into the living room. When he switched on the light she sprang from the nearest recliner, her urchin's face stretched in a wide grin. "Surprise."

At her sudden appearance, Martin caught his breath and Traveler's arm at the same time. "Good God. For a minute there I thought it was Kary."

"How did you get in?" Traveler asked.

The urchin's face grew up and smiled seductively. The woman that went with it hung on Traveler's free arm, tugging steadily as if in competition with Martin. She was dressed in white, a sleeveless blouse, slacks that showed no panty line, and sandals.

"I climbed through a back window to see you, Moroni." She rubbed a bony elbow where the skin had been scraped raw.

"That sounds like something Kary would have done," Martin grumbled.

Standing on tiptoe, she kissed Traveler's cheek. "I didn't have any choice. Moroni won't play fair."

"What kind of game is it?" Martin asked.

Claire opened her mouth to say something but made a face instead. Holding her nose she asked, "What is that God-awful smell?"

"Faith," Traveler answered.

"Don't pay attention to him," Martin said, and let go of his son to pull the asafetida bag from inside his shirt. "This is my magic charm."

Claire let go of her nose and Traveler backed up a step. "It makes me sick."

"I know how you feel. My stomach's been protesting for the last two hours." Martin stuffed the medicine pouch back inside his shirt. "Still, there are those who believe that this can cure whatever ails you. That being the case, what's the harm of a little stink between friends?"

"You're both crazy," she said.

Martin spread his hands in a gesture of goodwill. "As a father, I'm entitled to know how my son is mistreating you."

"He's supposed to find me when I'm lost."

"I've been telling him the same thing for years. Keep looking. Sooner or later you'll find the answers. Of course, they may not be what you expected."

Claire wrinkled her brow as if thinking that over. The wrinkles disappeared when she spoke. "A detective has to have clues, so I decided to bring him some myself since there was no one else to do it for me."

"I've never had much luck with clues," Martin said. "Every time I find them they prove something I didn't want to know."

She bit her lip.

"My advice is hire another detective," Martin added. "I told my wife the same thing once."

Traveler stared at his father, wondering what the occasion had been to offer such advice to Kary.

For a moment Claire didn't move or respond. Finally she smiled uncertainly and retrieved a small, beaded purse from the recliner where she'd been sitting in the dark. She handed the pocketbook to Traveler. "All the clues you'll need to find me are inside. Sometimes I think my soul could fit in there, too, along with the bits and pieces of my life, everything that's left of me after all these years."

Martin snorted. "You're still young. Practically a child."

"A woman's old the moment she has her first man."

She looked thinner than ever, Traveler noticed. Blue veins showed in her arms. The skin covering her face was stretched taut enough to reveal the skull underneath. As usual, she needed a man to feed upon. Once it had been he.

With a grin, Martin took her purse and opened it. It was filled with wads of paper.

"Those are my secret messages." Claire took back the purse and shook it, producing a jingling sound. "Bits and pieces, like I said. But you can't look at any of it until I leave. Those are the rules."

When she tried to give the purse to Traveler, he clasped his hands behind his back, an act that prompted one of her knowing smiles. Slowly and deliberately her accomplished tongue probed the red rim of her mouth. He closed his eyes but that only intensified the memories of her sexuality.

His eyes popped open. He felt short of breath.

"For Christ's sake," Martin said. "This could go on all night." He took the bag and placed it on the mantel next to a line of photographs that chronicled several generations of the Traveler family.

"Is that your wife?" Claire asked, touching a picture of Kary and Martin standing side by side in formal dress.

"That's what she called herself."

Claire smiled at Traveler. "We should have had our photo taken like that."

"We weren't married."

"I said the vows inside my head. God heard them even if you didn't."

Martin clapped his son on the back. "She's right, you know. She belongs up there beside your mother. It's like I said before, they're two of a kind. A matched pair."

Claire studied the photograph on the mantel more carefully.

"Women are the curse of us Travelers," Martin continued. "They're lost to us right from the start. We search for them constantly and all we ever find is unhappiness."

"You see," she said. "Your father understands the rules."

"Of course I do, my dear. You run along now and hide."

"And you'll send Moroni out to find me?"

"My son could never resist a clue, you should know that. Give him a few hours' sleep and he'll be hard at work, I assure you."

"What a dear old man you are." Her meager arms hugged Martin around the neck.

"You'll need a head start," he told her.

"You're perfect. Both of you." She threw herself at Traveler and kissed him on the lips before he had time to object. Her tongue teased once and then she was gone. Part of him, the part he distrusted, wanted to go after her.

Martin stared at the door long after it had closed behind her. Finally he said, "You need a place of your own if you're going to invite women over."

"I didn't invite her."

"How long have you been living here now? Six months, isn't it? Ever since you broke up with that woman. A man your age has got to start circulating again."

"You just said women were a curse."

"I also told Claire you'd come looking. But if you listened carefully I didn't say just who you'd be looking for."

"How can any of us know when to believe you?"

"The fact is, your being here is putting a crimp in my style, too." Martin fingered the asafetida bag through the material of his shirt. "If this goddamned stuff works, I just might find myself a rich widow to marry. Naturally I'm going to have a hell of time doing that with a grown son hanging around kibitzing."

Traveler didn't respond. He knew Martin too well.

Every few weeks his father would pretend to fly off the handle to give Traveler an easy way out of their relationship.

"I'm content living here for the moment."

"It ain't natural," Martin said, and stomped out of the room in a vain attempt to keep his satisfaction from showing.

Traveler sat down, avoiding the recliner that Claire had so recently occupied. There were times, he had to admit, when he longed for a place of his own. But now was not one of them. The tumor had seen to that.

He touched his own throat in sympathy. If only he could share some of Martin's pain. He'd do it gladly. It would be little enough payment for gaining a father who'd made childhood bearable by acting as a buffer against Kary's destructiveness.

"I'm leaving you," Kary had said, with five-year-old Moroni right there beside her as a witness. "Every time you look at me, Martin, you make me feel guilty."

"I'm sorry."

"I *am* guilty. I know that. But I don't like being constantly reminded of it with those sad looks of yours. Besides, it was your goddamned fault anyway. You should never have gone off and left me."

"There was a war."

"You were exempt. They weren't drafting policemen."

"They were drafting men ten years older than I was."

"You don't have to tell me what a hero you were. I read the papers."

"I did what I had to. That's all."

"That doesn't make the men who stayed behind cowards."

"I never said they were."

"I can see it in your eyes."

"You see more than I do."

"I didn't spread my legs for every four-effer who came along, you know."

"Don't talk that way in front of the boy."

"Why don't you call him Moroni? He's named for you, for God's sake. Or is that still bothering you? Have I tainted the Traveler bloodline?"

Martin sighed. "It was your idea to keep our home together when I came back."

"What choice did I have? Men walk away from their mistakes. Women get pregnant."

"How many mistakes are we talking about?"

"You agreed never to ask that."

"We shouldn't talk about any of this, Kary, not here and not now."

"I'm giving you a chance to say good-bye to Moroni. If you don't see him as your son, so be it."

"Where are you going?"

"To live with my parents."

"They follow the Word of Wisdom. You'll have to stop smoking and drinking. You'll have to go to church."

"I've been there before."

"And Moroni? You told me you didn't want him brought up to be LDS."

"I can change my mind."

"Have you asked *our* son what he wants?"

Kary stood up. "Come on, Moroni. Your grandparents are waiting."

"I have a right to visit my son."

"*Your* son."

"I've made him mine."

"Shall we tell him the truth?"

"You've been doing that for years." Martin knelt in front of Moroni. "It's not the beginning that counts with people, son. It's the way a man's raised that makes the difference."

"We'll see about that."

"I won't lose my son. I'll go to court if necessary."

"Damn you."

"I want him weekends."

"You'll have to pay support."

"All right."

"And money for me."

"Alimony?"

"There's not going to be any divorce, not to start with. We'll just call it spending money."

"How much?"

"As much as you can afford. That, or weekends are out."

"Very well."

Kary took Moroni's hand and jerked him toward the door.

"Take care of your mother," Martin called after them.

Traveler lived with his grandparents for two years. When Kary started talking about getting a divorce and remarrying, Traveler told her he wasn't going to live with a stranger and walked the five miles to the house on First Avenue. Kary moved back a week later.

23

Traveler was awakened the next morning by the distant sound of his father talking on the telephone. He grabbed the bedside extension and listened in.

"The biopsy report hasn't come back yet," Dr. Murphy was saying. "It ought to be here tomorrow or the next day."

"The day after tomorrow is the twenty-fourth," Martin reminded him.

"That's right. I forgot about Pioneer Days. No wonder everything's backed up."

"Damned Mormons."

"Take it easy, Martin. If I thought this delay was critical, I'd be there supervising the tests myself. You know that. I'll call you the moment I know anything."

"It's Moroni I'm worried about. He's fussing around here like a mother hen."

"I heard that," Traveler said.

"Detectives." The doctor snorted and hung up.

Traveler looked at his watch. It was after nine. "Hang up. I need to make a call."

"I already made it."

"Are you a mind-reader now?"

"That depends. My detective's curiosity started me wondering about Maria Gomez."

Traveler groaned. Martin was on the mark.

"She's still in jail. No bail. No visitors. Deportation pending."

"Any word from your sources on what the hell is going on?" Traveler asked.

"Someone's covering someone else's ass."

"But whose?"

"It won't make any difference to Maria. She's had it. I made another call, too. You remember Richard Lee. He runs a Mom-and-Pop in Little Mexico. Lee's Market. He told me Maria shops there, she and a friend. That would be the woman you told me about, Rosie."

"Did you wake up anybody else this morning?"

"Who'd you have in mind?"

"I thought maybe you might have a number for Heber Armstrong?"

"I'm working on it."

"How about working on breakfast?"

"You've got ten minutes before it starts getting cold."

"Shit," Traveler said, and headed for the shower.

Thirty minutes later Traveler drove his father to the Chester Building, temporarily pulling into the loading zone out front.

"You should have stayed home and rested," Traveler said.

"All I'd do is brood and maybe get drunk."

Traveler sighed deeply. He couldn't seem to get enough oxygen. "I thought I'd look over the site where Maria Gomez found the body."

"It's a bit late for that."

"Dad, you're the old pro when it comes to crime scenes. Come with me. I might miss something."

Martin rubbed his throat. "I don't know if it's my imagination or what. But I feel better this morning. The old gal's medicine bag must be working. The only trouble is, I'll have to stay upwind of everybody."

"I've gotten used to the smell."

"Like hell."

"So I lied. I still want you with me."

Martin laid a hand on Traveler's forearm. "I know you're trying to keep me busy. I appreciate the effort. But somebody's got to stay in the office once in a while."

"That's what answering machines are for."

"So maybe I'll walk around town and sightsee."

Traveler looked away from the pain in his father's eyes. Martin wasn't taking any chances on the biopsy report; he intended to make the rounds, saying good-bye to old friends and old haunts alike.

Martin forced a chuckle. "For once I've got something that smells worse than Barney Chester's cigars."

Up the street Mad Bill and Charlie Redwine turned the corner on Main and thumbed their noses at Brigham Young's statue in the intersection before starting down South Temple toward Traveler's car. Both men moved ponderously, as if wading through the heat waves rising from the sidewalk. The downtown temperature was ninety-four degrees. The air had a singed, ozone smell to it, as if lost souls were being raised from purgatory via baptism for the dead in the temple across the street.

Martin opened the door and stepped out onto the melting asphalt. "Look at Mad Bill, will you, wearing a sandwich board on a day like this."

Bill and Charlie arrived at curbside, both sweating profusely. The sandwich board read TITHE ACCEPTED HERE.

"I can smell them at ten paces," Martin whispered. "Barney won't let them in the door if I don't run interference with my asafetida."

"I'll be back as soon as I can."

"You're wasting your time. Murderers don't return to the scene of their crimes in this kind of weather."

24

Glendale Park is a long, narrow triangle of land bordered on two sides by water, the Surplus Canal on the west and the Jordan River on the east. Its squat, one-story recreation building, as grim and utilitarian as an LDS ward house, marked the center of an area that had been marked off with yellow, crime-scene tape. In front of the building stood a white metal pole, its flag at half-staff.

Though the murder was already forty-eight hours old, half a dozen uniformed officers were down on their hands and knees inside the taped barrier searching the grass. Outside the ribbon, a single policeman was doing his best to keep onlookers—children and their wide-eyed mothers, teenagers on summer vacation, and street people—from overrunning the site.

Traveler stayed in the car sudying his street map. Glendale Park, at Seventeenth South and Twelfth West, was about a mile and a half southwest of the most recent murder site, Jordan Park, whose western border was flanked by the Jordan River. Both were on the west side of town, in a deteriorating area that was fast being taken over by Orientals and Hispanics.

When sweat began dripping onto the map, he got out of the car and took a deep breath. The park air smelled of cottonwoods and mown grass. Yet asafetida lingered with him. To escape the thoughts it triggered, Traveler crossed the grass and joined the crowd.

His size drew looks of speculation, as if he might be there in some kind of official capacity.

"Do you know what they're looking for?" a woman ventured. She, like most of the other women, was wearing too much makeup, probably on the off-chance that television might decide to revisit the crime scene.

Traveler kept his comment to a shrug.

"Why don't they use dogs?"

A middle-aged man wearing the layered clothes of a hobo, the outermost of which was a red quilted vest, answered. "I read she was cut up into little pieces. And you know dogs. They gobble everything in sight."

"That's disgusting," the woman said, staring all the harder at the crawling policemen.

"A witness is being held in protective custody," Traveler ventured.

"I have a police scanner," the man said. "I got here as soon as the reporters and we didn't see anybody."

Traveler reassessed him. He was no hobo, though they'd become plentiful in Salt Lake in recent years. More likely he was a drug dealer who used a scanner to stay one jump ahead of the police. Or he could have been an undercover cop.

"There was a tarp over her," he went on. "But someone said she was naked underneath. It figures, if she was a hooker. They work this park at night, bringing their own blankets to save the cost of a motel room."

The *Tribune* had identified the victims, Alma Tucker, twenty, and Jan Gates, nineteen, as entertainers, an all-purpose euphemism in Mormon Country.

Traveler gossiped for another ten minutes but learned nothing of interest. Once back in his car, he switched the air conditioner to its maximum setting and headed north.

Cars were lined up to pass beneath the archway whose metal letters spelled out Jordan Park. As the scene of the most recent killing, still less than twenty-four hours old, it had drawn a bigger crowd than Glendale Park.

Traveler bypassed the entrance and continued up Ninth West toward Little Mexico, which had been known as Mormon Tokyo until the neighborhood changed a few years ago. The moment he stepped out of the Ford he could feel the eyeballs clicking his way. The hairs on the back of his neck prickled until he was well inside Lee's Market.

Richard Lee's dark skin and hair had enabled him to pretend to be half Oriental before the neighborhood's most recent ethnic evolution. Now he wore a white apron with Ricardo Lee embroidered on the front. Actually he qualified for membership in the Sons of the Utah Pioneers, since one of his relatives had accompanied Brigham Young on the trek from Nauvoo.

Lee was Martin's age. Both of them had been members of the University of Utah's tennis team.

At Traveler's entrance several shoppers left the store. Those already waiting to pay grew silent. Traveler got into line behind them and didn't speak until he and Lee were alone.

"My father sends his best."

Lee nodded in the direction of his disappearing customers and grinned. "They thought you were a cop. Come to think of it, you look like one."

He lunged across the counter to shake hands. "Ever since the killings we've had detectives in and out of here like clockwork. Now tell me about Martin. He didn't sound himself when we spoke on the phone this morning."

"His throat's bothering him."

"Tell him to take hot lemonade and vitamin C. If that doesn't work, add whiskey. It'll kill or cure."

"I'll do that."

"I still play tennis, you know. Remind him of that. Tell him I want a rematch as soon as he's feeling better. After all these years, maybe I can beat him for once."

"He gave it up."

"Why, for God's sake?"

Traveler had asked Martin the same question. His vague answer had been a smoke screen, behind which Traveler had sensed his mother's presence.

"You tell him to start practicing. A Lee won't be denied his chance at revenge."

Traveler nodded. "Since we're alone I'd like to ask some questions."

"Take your time. By now the word is out. I won't do any business until you're gone, not so much as a soda pop."

"You told Martin you knew Maria Gomez and her friend."

"Nice young women, both of them. Not typical, though. They came to this country to earn money honestly. When one of our local pimps tried to recruit them, they turned him down flat. That was right here in this store. I hate to think what might have happened if they'd said yes. They could have been killed, just like the woman in the Jordan Park. She was one of the pimp's working girls, using the name Jan Gates, as if that would fool anybody into thinking she wasn't Hispanic."

"It's Maria's friend, Rosie, I'm trying to locate."

"I hear things in this neighborhood. If I blab them around, I'll be out of business."

"Isn't there something you can do?"

"Not on that. I'm sorry."

"What about the pimp, then?"

"That's easy. His name is Garth Jensen. He hangs out at the Chi-Chi Club. Just wave the greenbacks and tell him you're a customer."

With blond hair, blue eyes, and dimpled chin, Garth Jensen looked like a cherub about to audition for the Mormon Tabernacle Choir. He eyed Traveler up and down and said, "If your cock's as big as the rest of you, I'm going to have to take out cunt insurance."

Traveler handed him a card.

"If you're not after a fuck, get out."

Traveler took back the card and replaced it with a twenty-dollar bill.

"Shee-yit." Jensen crumpled the bill and tossed it at the bartender, who caught and pocketed it in one smooth motion.

At the sight of Traveler the Chi-Chi Club, like Lee's Market, began to empty of what few noontime customers it had. Despite frigid and breezy air conditioning, the place reeked of sweat and stale beer.

"This is my turf," Jensen said. "What I say here goes. If I raise my finger, you're out on your ass."

Traveler looked around a room that was having trouble holding two pool tables. Except for the bartender, he and Jensen were alone.

When Traveler glared at the bartender, the man immediately raised his hands above counter level to show they were empty and began backing away. He kept right on going until he disappeared through a swinging door with a porthole window.

"Talk to me about Jan Gates."

Jensen licked his lips. "I don't care how big you are. You don't scare me."

Traveler grabbed a fistful of shirt with one hand and punched with the other. The pimp's eyes widened. His mouth opened and closed as he tried to suck air, but the muscles of his diaphragm were momentarily paralyzed. As a linebacker, Traveler had gone through the same kind of agony when sucker-punched by offensive linemen.

He released his grip and the pimp slid off his stool and onto the sawdusted floor, where his face started turning blue. When his legs began to thrash, Traveler took hold of his belt and worked him up and down like a bellows.

Jensen started breathing and got sick at the same time. Once the retching stopped, Traveler rolled him to a relatively clean spot on the floor and knelt beside him.

"The second time is worse. Your lungs feel like they're on fire. You think you're never going to breathe again. Sometimes you don't."

"You're a bastard like the rest of them," Jensen croaked.

"Are you speaking in the plural?"

"Did they send you to check up on me?"

"What do you think?"

"Go back and tell them I haven't said a thing."

"But you will." Traveler pushed his fist forward until it touched Jensen's nose.

The pimp's eyes lost focus. "I'm living up to our bargain. You tell them that. Please."

"Whose bargain?"

"Jesus and Mary. What have I done?"

Traveler dragged the pimp to his feet and set him down on the bar stool once again. "We can pretend we're bowling. You're the pin. I set you up and knock you down."

Jensen shrugged. "If I open my mouth to you, I don't survive. Not in this town. Do your worst. I'm probably a dead man already and don't know it."

"I'll tell you what. I'll give you a head start."

Jensen glanced toward the door. "They sent you to kill me, didn't they?"

"You said you were dead already."

The pimp backed toward the exit. When he got there he shouted, "You're a fucking pussy. A couple of more punches and I would have told you everything."

With that, he turned and ran. Traveler didn't bother chasing him. He figured he already knew what Garth Jensen was afraid of.

25

Gesturing frantically, Barney Chester dashed from behind the cigar counter and grabbed Traveler's arm. "There are cops waiting for you upstairs." His voice soared with excitement.

Traveler allowed himself to be pulled out of line of sight with the elevator, where Nephi Bates was listening to the Mormon Tabernacle Choir with his eyes closed, and into an alcove that held two old-fashioned phone booths and the entrance to the men's room. Blocking all three doors were Mad Bill and Charlie, both sitting cross-legged on the marble floor and rolling a pair of handmade cigarettes.

"Goddamn it. That had better be tobacco." Barney's voice sounded distorted because of the cigar clenched between his teeth.

"Peyote is legal for Indians," Bill said. "It's part of their religion. As for prophets like myself, who's to say what's lawful?"

With a flourish Charlie struck a wooden kitchen match on the marble floor and lit up. The smoke ring he blew at Barney's head disintegrated just as it was about to become a halo.

Barney backed up a step. "That shit will get you sent to jail, not heaven. There are cops are all over the place today."

"That's not funny," Bill said.

"They're after me," Traveler explained.

Charlie doused his cigarette with spit and then swallowed the evidence.

Barney said, "Get that Indian out of here before he throws up on my floor."

"Don't worry," Bill said. "Charlie's done it before. Instead of getting sick, he talks to his gods. Sometimes he lets his Sandwich Prophet listen in."

As if on cue the Indian's eyes rolled into his head, leaving only the bloodshot whites behind. Traveler suspected it was part of a well-rehearsed scam, though to what end he couldn't guess.

Barney held out his hand toward Bill, palm up. "I don't want you in a trance, too. Now give me that cigarette."

Bill struck a match against his sandwich board. "A couple of puffs. That's all I ask." He, too, began blowing smoke rings. Only his were too ragged to look like haloes.

Figuring relaxation by proxy couldn't hurt, Traveler took a deep breath. "How many cops are there?"

"Three at first," Barney said without taking his eyes off Bill. "Two uniforms and a detective."

"And now?"

"Damn it, Bill," Barney said, ignoring Traveler's question. "You're stretching my patience. Either you get rid of that, or you and Charlie are out on the street."

The Sandwich Prophet took one last puff. "Anything you say, Barney. You want me to flush it down the toilet?"

"That would be nice."

Bill helped the white-eyed Indian to his feet and then pounded him on the back. The impact jiggled Charlie's pupils back into place.

"I am a Lamanite," Charlie said. "The lost tribe of Israel."

"Come on. It's time to take a pee."

Bill led his Navajo disciple into the men's room. As soon as the door closed behind them, Barney took a fresh cigar from his shirt pocket and lit up. Once he had it going properly he moved around the alcove, blowing smoke into every corner to camouflage the marijuana.

Finally he sagged against the wall and grinned. "To think that you, a man named after an angel, is about to get himself arrested." He held out his hands like a criminal awaiting handcuffs. "Is your life flashing before your eyes, Moroni?"

"You're stalling, Barney. Who else is upstairs?"

"I tried to stop them, but they showed me a warrant."

"Who, Barney?"

"That so-called friend of yours from the Hotel Utah."

"Willis Tanner?"

"The way he walked in here, you'd think he was one of the Twelve Apostles."

"What's the charge against me?"

"I don't know. I guess I should have read the warrant, huh?"

Traveler edged around the corner of the alcove until he could see the rest of the lobby. No one had come in after him, and there was no sign of a police car in the street outside. Even so, three cops and Willis Tanner added up to more than assault on a pimp.

"I'd better go up and see what they want."

"I've got a better idea. Bill's always said he wanted to be a martyr. Now's his chance."

Barney pushed open the door to the men's room. "Step out here, William. Sainthood is at hand."

Mad Bill and Charlie, both of whom had splashed cold water over themselves, dripped across the alcove to where Barney stood.

"The police are waiting upstairs to arrest Moroni," he told them. "Willis Tanner is with them."

Bill placed a wet hand on Traveler's head as if giving benediction. " 'Behold, we are surrounded by demons, yea, we are encircled about by the angels of him who hath sought to destroy our souls.' "

"That's him," Barney said.

"Religion is a dangerous business, Moroni. I've told you that before."

Barney's head bobbed. "Exactly. That's why we want you to go upstairs first and find out what's happening."

"To hell with that," Traveler said.

"Like Daniel, I'll go into the lion's den."

"Don't be a fool," Charlie said. "I'll go. If they try anything with me, I'll have every civil rights lawyer in town on their asses."

Traveler blinked in surprise. The Indian was usually a man of few words.

"The lost tribe of Israel is about to be found," Charlie added, and dashed toward the stairs before Traveler could stop him.

Ten minutes later, a pair of burly policemen led Charlie away in handcuffs.

"I must follow my disciple," Bill said. "Take care of my sandwich board."

Without waiting for an answer, he hurried across the lobby and out through the revolving door.

Anger rose inside Traveler with a rush. He stepped into one of the phone booths and dialed his own office.

Willis Tanner answered.

"I expect Charlie Redwine to be released immediately." Traveler's voice was flat and cold.

"Anything you say, Mo."

"You can release Maria Gomez while you're at it."

"I have to see you."

"So you can have me arrested?"

"That was a mistake. I realize that now. There's a better way. Meet me somewhere. That's all I ask."

Traveler thought that over for a moment. Willis Tanner could not be trusted when the church was involved. Still, Traveler had to gamble if he wanted information.

"All right, Willis. We'll meet at our old hideout in one hour."

"We were kids when we built that place."

Exactly, Traveler thought. He still remembered every nook and cranny, every escape route. Ambushing him there would be that much more difficult.

26

The Tanner family lived on U Street, around the corner from Traveler's house. The backyards of both properties met for a distance of about fifty feet, most of it taken up by two rickety garages. Willis had broken his arm once trying a Superman leap, complete with dish-towel cape, from one garage roof to another. After that he and Traveler decided a lean-to was safer and scrounged two-by-fours and plywood to build a clubhouse, using garage walls as support. Their hideout had two old carpet pieces as hanging doors and could be entered from either property.

In recent years a row of fast-growing junipers had masked one backyard from the other, and Traveler had no idea whether the lean-to was still there. The chances were against it, though Willis's widowed mother still lived in the same house. She, he remembered, had disapproved of him as much as Martin had frowned on Willis.

Traveler arrived early, intending to scout the neighborhood. But when he tried to squeeze through a narrow gap in a fence, the secret passage of twelve-year-olds, he knew it was hopeless. If Willis Tanner wanted him arrested badly enough, he could supplement the police force with an army of deacons from hundreds of LDS wards throughout the city.

He vaulted the fence, strode down the Tanner's driveway, and knocked on the front door. When Loreta Tanner opened it she condemned Traveler with the same shake of her head she'd been using on him for thirty years. Her hair had gone from gray to white in recent years. She seemed to be shrinking, too, an impression enhanced by a faded housedress that hung like a larger woman's hand-me-down.

"You've gotten bigger," she said. "But you haven't changed. I can see that in your face."

"I'm supposed to meet Willis here."

"I never liked having you in my house, even when you were a boy. You smelled of cigarettes."

"Could I help it if my mother smoked?"

"She's been raised, you know. Willis showed me the printouts. One of her cousins did the baptism."

Latter-day Saints in good standing performed baptisms for the dead on departed relatives who'd failed to see the light themselves. Without such ceremonies there was no entry to God's exclusively Mormon heaven.

"Knowing my mother, she'd probably prefer it in purgatory."

"That's blasphemy."

"The truth usually is."

"You'll never be raised. Willis and I will see to that."

"Thank you."

Her eyes narrowed. "Don't just stand there. You're letting the heat in. And me an old lady suffering from heat rash at that."

"Yes, ma'am." Traveler stepped across the threshold and closed the door behind him.

The house smelled the same as he remembered, a mixture of furniture polish and simmering vegetables, which Mrs. Tanner had grown in what she called her Victory Garden, though the war was long gone. The living room also looked unchanged, a trio of overstuffed chairs from the 1940s, each with its own floor lamp, a sofa that dated from the depression, and Mrs. Tanner's pride and joy, an upright piano on which Willis had practiced every day after school, thereby delaying many a touch-football game.

"My son called me just before you got here. He told me to go out and look in that old shed you two built next to the garage. If you weren't there, he said, I was to leave a note telling you to wait inside the house for him."

Her head shook, half tremor, half condemnation. " 'I'll do no such thing,' I told him. 'I've got better things to do than worry about heathen gentiles. If he comes to the door, that's another matter. But I'm not carrying notes in this heat.' "

She took a pair of rimless glasses from the gleaming piano top and adjusted them on her nose. "Let me get a better look at you." Her tongue made a clucking noise. "Naming you Moroni was an abomination."

"My mother gets full credit for that. Maybe she shouldn't have been raised after all."

"I think it would be best if you waited in the basement."

Willis's room had been in the basement, next to the furnace. The only windows were narrow and barred.

"It seems like yesterday when you two used to play down there," she added, her voice softening at the memory. "Do you remember?"

He said that he did.

"I used to worry that you'd lead my boy astray."

Actually, it was Willis who'd procured their first pack of cigarettes. And girlie magazines. Though where he'd gotten them Traveler couldn't imagine, then or now.

"Thank God you couldn't tempt him away from the church."

"Was it Willis's suggestion that I trap myself in the basement?"

She led him down a central hall and into the kitchen, where she stopped in front of the cellar door.

"His toys are still in the closet downstairs." Her tone seemed to suggest that Traveler might want to take them out and play with them again. "He likes to come here and relax sometimes. That's why I keep the room ready for him."

When Traveler opened the basement door a draft of cool air rushed up the stairs, carrying with it the smell of earth and dusty concrete. His hand remembered the light switch. When he threw it the naked bulb was like a memory beacon. He followed it down the stairs, conscious with each step that he could be descending into a trap.

Willis's room had never been completely finished. The ceiling was nothing more than cross-beams and subflooring. One concrete wall stopped at chest height, leaving an open crawl space through which drafts whistled constantly. That space had also provided innumerable hiding places for boyhood contraband.

The same flowered rug lay on the red cement floor. On top of it stood the chest of drawers that Traveler had helped paint bright green, and the narrow metal bed, which had shed its color almost as quickly as they applied it. The only thing new in the room, as far as he could remember, was a telephone and a nineteen-inch color TV set, both resting on a chrome stand with a VCR shelf beneath it.

Ignoring spider webs, Traveler boosted himself onto the retaining wall to check the nearest of their secret hiding places. When his fingers touched paper he carefully retrieved one of the girlie magazines Willis had shared with him. Opening its pages was like going back in time. The women who'd titillated their youth showed less skin than daytime television.

Old guilt caused Traveler to hide the magazine when he heard footsteps on the stairs. Tanner's feet came into view first. There appeared to be no one with him.

"Did you leave the police upstairs?"

"This is all I brought with me." Tanner stepped into the basement carrying a videotape player. "Let me get this hooked up and we're in business."

He slipped the VCR onto the shelf under the TV set and

began screwing cable connectors into place. Once that was done, he switched on the set. When the picture flared to life on a game show, he muted the sound and turned around to face Traveler.

"You're not authorized to see what I'm about to show you. It could cost me my job, Mo. It might even get me excommunicated."

Traveler searched his friend's face for signs of treachery. All that was visible was his nervous squint. Traveler said, "You've been working for the church ever since college. My bet is that you've never done anything without authorization in all that time."

A tick pulled at Tanner's eye. He covered it with one hand and pointed with the other. "Let's say you're right. Some kinds of authorizations are never put in writing or given in front of witnesses. It's my ass that's going to get burned if you leak any of this."

"When you use language like that I get nervous." Traveler sat down on the metal bed, causing a protesting squeak of springs.

"I'm making a point. I want you to know that I'm putting myself in your hands. If we weren't friends, you'd be in jail right now."

"Sure."

"Go ahead and scoff. I had the warrant and you know it." Tanner half turned, his finger poised over the VCR's start button. "When you see this, you'll know I'm a man who pays his debts."

He hit the button and cranked up the volume. The game show gave way to a long shot of a park with children at play. Some were on swings, some on teeter-totters. Still others were jumping rope. The sound of their laughter mixed with the wind hissing into a microphone. Traveler recognized the area near the tennis courts at Liberty Park, the biggest picnic and recreational area in downtown Salt Lake.

The camera began to zoom, closing in on a group of

young girls skipping rope. Accompanying the zoom was a rustling, staticlike sound, as if the off-camera microphone was being clumsily redirected.

After a moment, the girl's singsong chant became clear. "Bread and butter, sugar and spice, how many boys think I'm nice? One, two, three, four . . ."

The girl jumping made a mistake. The chanting stopped while she untangled herself and exchanged places with one of the girls who'd been twirling the rope.

"Sugar and cream, bread and butter, what is the name of my true lover? A, B, C, D . . ."

A man's voice, one that has been electronically distorted, overrode the singing. "They're young now, maybe even innocent. But not for long. Like all of their kind, they're destined to become whores. 'Woe unto them who commit whoredoms, for they shall be thrust down into hell.'"

Tanner punched the pause button. "I looked that up. It's from *The Book of Mormon.* Two Nephi, nine:thirty-six."

He restarted the tape. The camera moved on, focusing on first one girl and then another. "'And the great and abominable church, which is the whore of all the earth, shall be cast down by devouring fire.'"

Again Tanner stopped the videotape. "That's Doctrine and Covenants, Mo. The words of Joe Smith."

He ground his teeth before jabbing the button once again. On screen the children were replaced by a montage of women's faces. They were young and good-looking. Judging by the shakiness of the camera and telephoto distortion, they'd been videotaped at a great distance.

"And I am that devouring fire."

Tanner froze the picture. "Do you recognize her?"

Traveler shook his head.

"Alma Tucker, the first one to be killed."

Breathing noisily through his mouth, Tanner concentrated on manipulating buttons, easing the picture forward frame by frame. "Here's number two. Juanita Sanchez, alias Jan Gates. Now watch closely. I'm going to let them roll for a while."

Female faces flashed by in ever-shorter bursts. Traveler blinked. One of them looked like Claire.

"Stop the tape and rerack it."

"Don't worry, she's coming up again."

Tanner caught Claire in freeze frame.

"Notice the background," Tanner said. "It's your house. Your front porch."

Traveler lurched from the bed to get a closer look at the screen. "That tape has a professional look to it. The editing is a hell of a lot better than most home movies."

"That's what our people say, too, though his long shots leave something to be desired. Of course, he was probably trying to hide the camera from his subjects."

Victims, Traveler thought. The word was victims. "Claire showed up at the house yesterday. Whoever took this must have been waiting across the street."

"Or following her."

Traveler caught his breath. He should have thought of that. "Is there anything else I ought to know?"

"Unfortunately, yes." Tanner sighed. His shoulders slumped. When he pushed the playback button his trembling finger had a hard time hitting the mark.

The little girls were back, jumping rope. Their singsong cry rose, then faded. The narrator's contrived voice overrode them with heavy breathing. Then he spoke. "A hundred years ago the children of London sang a different song."

He sang, his voice an electronically exaggerated falsetto. "Jack the Ripper's dead, and lying on his bed. He cut his throat with Sunlight Soap. Jack the Ripper's dead."

A rumble of distorted laughter brought gooseflesh crawling up Traveler's spine.

"The little whores are lying. Jack's not dead. Jack's back."

27

Tanner had tears in his eyes. "We're two days away from celebrating the rebirth of God's chosen people. You realize that, don't you, Moroni? The moment when God led Brigham Young to this, our promised land. And now the Devil has sent his disciple among us to test our faith."

"This guy is obviously crazy."

"But who made him that way? Surely not God."

"We'd better go back and look at that tape again. Count how many women are on it."

Tanner shook his head. "There's no need. The count is ten. The original Jack the Ripper killed five."

"Maybe he intends to double the record." Or maybe, Traveler thought, the number ten was a diversion. If you counted Pioneer Day itself, there were three days to go. Three days and three more victims would equal Jack the Ripper's count.

"Claire's the only other face on the tape that we've identified so far. If I hadn't recognized her, we'd have no leads at all, though we are checking all known prostitutes, since they were Jack's original targets."

"Claire doesn't qualify," Traveler said. "She never does anything for money."

"Would a maniac make that kind of distinction?"

Traveler thought that over for a moment. "I'd better

warn her." He picked up the phone. "Is this an extension?"

"My mother can't listen in, if that's what you mean."

Traveler dialed a number he knew by heart, but which he had never intended to use. He let it ring a long time before giving up.

"We can't allow this man to come to trial," Tanner went on. "You understand that, don't you?"

"You have to catch him first."

Tanner shrugged his shoulders as if to say that was a forgone conclusion.

"Goddamn it, Willis. I want to know what's going on in that Mormon mind of yours."

"I can't say."

"Won't, you mean."

He shrugged again.

"Has something happened to Claire?" Traveler grabbed the front of Tanner's shirt and lifted him on to tiptoe. Cloth ripped. A button popped loose and rolled on the concrete.

"The truth is, we'd like to hire you, Mo."

"Sure. And how would you like him killed?"

"It doesn't have to come to that. Committing him somewhere would be acceptable, as long as we're certain that he can't sell his story to Hollywood."

"What about Claire?" Traveler said.

"I didn't have to show you the tape, you know."

"If you wanted my help, you did."

"I have no reason to believe that she's come to any kind of harm. Now let go of me, damn it."

Traveler tossed him onto the bed. "You have a suspect in mind, don't you?"

"We have a short list. We think he's on it."

Traveler slapped himself on the forehead. "What a dummy. You told me that once before, missionaries like Heber Armstrong who've gone astray."

"Unfortunately he isn't the only one on our list who's had some kind of television training."

"What kind of proof do you have that your Jack the Ripper is a missionary?"

"Ex-missionary." Tanner squirmed. His lips pressed together. But before he could say anything further, the pager attached to his belt beeped its alarm.

One side of his face twitched. He groaned, picked up the phone, and then turned his back so he could punch in numbers without Traveler seeing them."

"This is Tanner, sir. My verification number is 447769." He cast a quick glance at Traveler. "That should be changed after this call."

As Tanner listened one side of his face puckered until his squint resembled a Halloween mask. His entire body was trembling by the time he hung up.

"Liberty Park," he said. "There's been another killing."

28

Liberty Park is home to one of the oldest structures in Salt Lake, the Isaac Chase House, a two-story adobe built in 1852, a pioneer shrine now turned into a monument to murder. A cordon of police had the place surrounded. They, in turn, were surrounded by trees, elms and cottonwoods, sucked limp by the heat.

The park had been one of Traveler's boyhood haunts. He'd picnicked there, ridden the merry-go-round, and watched fireworks shows on both Independence days, the nation's on July 4 and the Mormons' on July 24. But now, as he and Willis Tanner pushed through the sightseers and crossed the grass toward the shrouded body, the scene looked as unreal as a backdrop at a high school play.

The cast of characters, headed by the chief of police, a captain, and two lieutenants, were glaring at him. Only one man, so elderly he was leaning heavily on a cane, smiled. The smile made him look vaguely familiar.

"That's Ephraim Moyle," Tanner murmured.

Moyle, in a lightweight gray suit, white shirt, and black silk tie, could have been mistaken for an undertaker. But Traveler knew better. He was one of the Twelve Apostles, right-hand man to Elton Woolley, president of the church. As such Moyle was rumored to be next in line, the future prophet, through whom God would speak as He had through Joseph Smith in the beginning.

Traveler slowed. His father was right. Never mix work and the Mormon Church. Men like Moyle and Elton Woolley had more power than the president of the United States. They weren't bound by man's law, but by God's, and that they interpreted for themselves by revelation.

"Come on," Tanner whispered. He took hold of Traveler's elbow and applied forward pressure. "It was Moyle I spoke to on the phone."

Moyle must have heard the comment, because he widened his smile and beckoned Traveler to join him.

"Be good," Tanner mouthed like a stiff-lipped ventriloquist.

Though wobbling on his cane, Moyle reached out to shake hands. "Moroni Traveler. I've been waiting to meet you." His eyes were bright, his voice firm and youthful. "Elton Woolley told me the name suits you. He's right. I left him within the hour."

"Apostle Moyle lives in the Hotel Utah next door to our prophet," Tanner explained.

"My wife is dead," Moyle went on. "I have no family."

The police chief and his staff backed off to a discreet distance.

Traveler forced a smile of his own. Most likely Woolley's name was being used as a lever, or maybe a carrot. But tempting carrots tended to have big sticks attached to them. Besides which, it was much safer to remain as anonymous as possible in a theocracy like Utah.

Moyle turned his smile on Tanner. "Have you told Moroni everything?"

Tanner's jaw fell open. "I didn't have clearance to go that far."

"But surely you've explained why we need his help so badly?"

Tanner went through a ticklike contortion that verged on genuflection.

Moyle sighed unhappily. "We need more than your help, Moroni. We need your faith." One of his bright blue eyes winked. "Don't look so worried. I'm not here to proselytize. Your belief in justice will suffice for the moment, not that we won't win you over in the end."

"Amen," Tanner said.

Moyle raised his cane to point at the body. "Before we say anything else, I think you ought to take a look at the dead woman."

Traveler cast a quick glance at the black plastic shroud. Peering beneath it was the last thing he wanted to do.

"I understand that a woman you know was on the videotape," Moyle said. "So I realize you have a personal stake in this. I'll wait for you in the car."

The comment left the apostle short of breath. He reached out to Tanner, who immediately offered his arm for support. Together they walked slowly past the waiting police officers and toward a gray limousine with darkened windows.

Moyle must have said something to the officers on the way by, because the chief himself hurried over to remove the shroud.

Traveler caught his breath. Despite the savagery confronting him, he felt a surge of relief. It wasn't Claire. At the same time he was ashamed of his reaction, and angry. The attack had been so viciously sexual, as if the killer had been trying to cut out an erogenous malignancy.

A sheet of paper protruded from her ruined vagina.

He swallowed the bile rising in his throat and leaned down to read the words that were written in blood.

The angels' share.

A fresh wave of nausea rocked him. The chief snatched him out of harm's way.

"Is there anything else I can do for you, sir?" the man said through clenched teeth, his disapproval of outsiders obvious in both tone and expression.

Traveler started to explain his presence. But there was no point. He didn't give a damn what the police thought. He couldn't walk away from the case now, not when the possibility existed that Claire might be the next victim.

The taste in his mouth was as sour as his mood by the time he joined Ephraim Moyle in the backseat of the air-conditioned limousine. Tanner was sitting in the front, staring straight ahead but obviously listening, whether as a witness or an eavesdropper Traveler couldn't say.

"Events like this serve a purpose," the old man said. "They teach us that we must remain vigilant. We dare not stray from God's light, because Lucifer is waiting for us in the darkness."

Traveler leaned back and closed his eyes. But the dead girl was waiting for him. He blinked, focusing on the back of Tanner's sweating neck.

"The angels' share," Moyle said. "Do you understand its significance?"

"No more than Maria Gomez did."

Moyle dismissed the criticism with a shake of his head. "The same message has been left with each victim."

A sigh rattled in the apostle's throat. "It is a judgment upon us. If we cannot send out our missionaries to spread the word of God, we are lost."

Tanner's head bowed as if in prayer.

"It goes back to the very beginning of our church. In 1840 Joseph Smith himself sent Brigham Young on a mission to England. We were a poor lot in those days. The poor can't pay a tithe when they have nothing. Brigham knew that. Tradition says that he came up with a solution. 'I'll pay my tithe in converts. That will be my angels' share.' Of course, we don't have any of this in writing, you understand. But it has become part of our training ritual. 'Go out and collect the angels' share,' we tell each and every one of our missionaries."

"Heber Armstrong went to England," Traveler pointed out.

"So did the others on our list."

"Have they gone missing, too?"

"Only their faith is gone." Moyle drew a quick breath. "We have watched them for several days now, long enough to narrow the field. Only Heber Armstrong remains unaccounted for."

"If you know all this, why do you need me?"

The apostle lowered his head until his chin was resting on his chest. "Because Claire Bennion is on the tape, Willis and I believe that the killer may have singled you out. Perhaps he has something against you personally."

"If Armstrong is in town, he probably knows I'm looking for him by now."

"The name he goes by makes no difference. It's us, the LDS Saints, that Satan is after. He wants company in hell." The word hell triggered Traveler's memory. *I am a missionary of the damned,* Armstrong had written to his fiancée. Even so, Traveler thought it unlikely that a missing missionary had evolved into Jack the Ripper.

"What kind of motive could he have?" he asked.

"Satan is like a vampire who feeds on souls."

"Maybe your missionary met another woman. It happens, you know. Maybe he thought it was easier to disappear than to come home and explain."

"This could be political." Moyle pulled at the loose skin beneath his chin.

"If he lost faith . . ."

"If Satan took it from him, you mean," the apostle interrupted.

". . . he might not enjoy the idea of making such a revelation to his parents and girlfriend."

Moyle dismissed the suggestion with a flick of his hand. "If this is political, one of those fundamentalist sects is most likely behind it. You know the kind. The ones who keep plaguing us with new revelations on polygamy."

Traveler looked toward the body, which was again uncovered and being examined by someone from the coroner's office. "That wasn't the work of conspirators."

"We depend on the tithe for survival," Moyle went on. "We cannot afford to have this killer, or killers, sow seeds of distrust."

"My worry is Claire, not theology."

"Based on Willis's recommendation, I have spoken to the prophet about you, Moroni. He and I agree that you will work for us."

"I have a client."

"You have a responsibility."

"You have an army at your disposal."

"They haven't found him yet," Moyle said.

"And the police?"

"The chief is coordinating for us. But we don't want the specifics spreading to the rank and file."

"I'm one man, for God's sake. What chance would I have?"

"Maybe none at all. But you have motivation, Moroni. Sometimes that's better than faith. Now, if you'll hand me the contract, Willis, Mr. Traveler and I will seal our bargain."

A clipboard appeared instantly. The form attached to it was blank except for a line at the bottom.

"It's merely a precaution," Moyle said. "We have to be certain that you'll keep our secrets."

"I intend to cooperate," Traveler said, thinking of Claire. "But I'm not about to sign something like that."

"All right, Willis, you can honk the horn."

As soon as Tanner complied, police surrounded the limousine.

"You won't be able to find Miss Bennion if you're in jail."

Traveler clenched his fists to keep from grabbing the old man and shaking him. "You bastard."

Moyle pushed the button that lowered the window next to Traveler. "Take a look at that poor girl out there. Imagine something like that happening to your Claire."

"Willis knows better than to threaten me."

"Of course. He's told me all about you. But you see, there's something else you don't know. We think Claire's been kidnapped."

Traveler's hands were shaking so badly he could hardly sign his name.

29

Claire had moved since she and Traveler lived together. Her new apartment was on Second Avenue, between A and B streets, in a neighborhood on its way to becoming fashionable again after decades of neglect. He'd been aware of her location for some time but had never intended to make use of the knowledge.

Her building had a notice out front that said it was the future home of Temple-view Townhouse Condominiums, though as far as he could see there was no view at all.

The downstairs door was propped open for ventilation but the smell infesting the lobby—the stale residue of half a century—was immune to fresh air. Breathing through his mouth, Traveler climbed the stairs and knocked on the door of 2C. A three-by-five card had been tacked next to a doorbell wearing so many coats of paint its button had disappeared. Press-on letters spelled out *Claire's Place.*

He knocked again. When he got no answer, he lowered his shoulder and gradually applied pressure until the dead bolt ripped through the door's rotting frame.

He was inside, the door closed quietly behind him, before he realized he wasn't seeing himself in a mirror. It was a life-size blow-up, taken when he was still playing professional football for Los Angeles. The silver uniform was stained with grass and blood, the helmet scuffed from years of impact as a linebacker.

The photograph took up what wall space there was in a tiny entrance hall. When Traveler stepped into the living room he found himself facing a larger wall that was covered with poster-sized action shots. Judging by the graininess of the pictures, enlargements must have been made from photos that appeared in sports magazines.

A newspaper headline had been taped across one of the posters: L.A. LINEBACKER CRIPPLES RUNNING BACK.

He ignored an urge to rip it from the wall and searched the apartment. Nothing seemed to be disturbed or missing. Under normal circumstances he wouldn't have been alarmed. Claire often disappeared, sometimes without taking so much as a change of clothes with her. Usually she ended up telephoning Traveler for help, begging him to follow the clues and come find her. There was a purse full of them at the house right now. But they were useless if Ephraim Moyle was to be believed, not to mention Willis Tanner, who'd come running after Traveler when he walked away from the apostle's limousine a few minutes earlier. "Listen to me, Mo. I couldn't help it. I had you watched. That's how we know about the kidnapping. We saw it happen when she left your place. We had no reason to worry about her safety then, so I didn't send one of my Tongans to watch you, only a young deacon. There was nothing he could do when someone forced her into a car last night."

"Did she know you were watching her?"

"I have no idea," Tanner had said.

Thinking about it now, Traveler wondered if a fake kidnapping was another of Claire's games. Actually, it didn't matter. He'd have to assume the worst. Which was exactly what Claire would have thought, too.

He searched the apartment more thoroughly, hoping to come up with one of her written clues. When that didn't happen, he decided to check the nearest bar, which also happened to be her favorite, The Beehive.

Utah is known as the beehive state. In Salt Lake City alone, there are beehive appliance stores, candy companies, brick yards, pizza parlors, bail bondsmen, just about anything imaginable, all because early Mormons saw bees as a special manifestation of nature. They were industrious and cooperative, producing honey from the desert wilderness, just as the faithful intended to do one day.

The Beehive Bar & Grill was on South Temple Street, only a few blocks up from Brigham Young's personal residence, the Beehive House, where he had lived with his favorite wife of the moment. The rest of his wives had stayed two doors away in the Lion House.

When Traveler entered the bar, the female bartender glared at him and pointed a clawlike, red-nailed finger. "I recognize you. You're not welcome here."

The place was long and narrow, like a railroad flat. The only light came from a spotlight buried in the ceiling above the cash register and two glowing neons that advertised Coors and Hamms.

A solitary drinker sitting in front of the cash register swiveled his head and squinted at Traveler.

"His name's Moroni," the bartender said. She was hennaed and heading into an overweight middle age.

"No angels allowed," her counter customer replied.

"He's the one Claire talks about."

"The one she calls all the time?"

"That's right. The one who lets her down."

"Yeah. The goddamned football hero."

"I need your help," Traveler said to the woman.

"I'll give you the same kind of help you've dished out to Claire. None. Now get out of here."

"I think she's in trouble."

"She's been that way for a long time, thanks to you."

An explanation would have made things worse. "I think she's missing for real this time."

"Then you should be out looking for her."

"What's the problem, Frieda?" someone called from a shadowy back booth.

Traveler blinked. His eyes still hadn't adjusted fully to the Beehive's dim interior.

"I want this guy out of here," Frieda said.

One shape emerged from the booth, then another and another. When they entered the Hamms' blue glow, Traveler knew he was in trouble. They were big, not as big as he was, but big enough and shiny-eyed drunk enough to think three-to-one odds were all they needed. To win, he'd have to hurt one of them badly with the first punch, break a bone so the other two would get jelly-leg and back off. He felt a small satisfying glow of rage growing within him. It needed only the slightest excuse to blossom into mindless violence.

He left the bar without another word.

"Coward," someone shouted after him.

Since his locked car stood at the curb outside, he had no choice but to turn and stand his ground when the door pushed open behind him. A face peeked out, went wide-eyed at the sight of him in daylight, and abruptly disappeared back inside.

"Coward," the voice repeated, but in a tone of obvious relief.

Driving away, the word kept echoing inside his head. Claire had called him a coward once, too, the culmination of a Sunday afternoon drive that ended at the Lagoon Resort north of town. The trip out Interstate 15 had taken only a few minutes. Along the way he kept looking for his youth, for old Highway 89, which he'd traveled so often with his father in their '41 Packard, making a game out of reading the billboards out loud as they went. *Swim in water fit to drink*, the Lagoon posters had said.

"I want to start with the roller-coaster," Claire announced the moment they were through the gate. "I need to feel like a girl again."

But she caught sight of the Fun House first and began dancing around Traveler like an anxious child. "Please, Daddy. Please," she cried in her best little-girl voice.

Embarrassed, he hustled her inside where she bypassed the mirrors to lose herself in the maze.

"Find me, find me," she kept calling.

But no matter how fast he moved, she eluded him. He didn't catch up with her for nearly an hour. By then she was at the refreshment stand, eating a hot dog and hanging on the arm of a greasy-haired young man with anchor tattoos on his biceps. He was as thin as Claire, with glittery eyes that said he'd been drinking. Eyes contemptuous of Traveler's size.

"Is this the fucking angel you were telling me about?"

"The Angel Moroni," she said, nodding vigorously. "Here to save our souls."

"I'm going home," Traveler said so softly that it didn't sound like his voice. "Are you coming?"

"You big bastards are all alike. A bunch of fucking pansies."

Traveler turned his back and started to walk away, unwilling to repeat the kind of violence that Claire had maneuvered him into once before. He sensed, or maybe heard, the swinging catsup bottle. He ducked. The bottle raked his ear, setting the side of his head on fire with pain.

"If you want me," Claire said, "you have to fight for me."

Traveler swung around in time to catch the second, bone-jarring blow on his forearm. The man grunted in surprise. The catsup bottle went flying, splattering glass and goo over the asphalt.

He aimed a kick at Traveler's groin. When Traveler dodged to one side, the man lost his balance and toppled into Traveler's grasp.

"Hurt him," she cried.

Traveler lifted him overhead like a barbell.

"Make him bleed."

Traveler resisted the urge to throw the man at her, dumping him in a puddle of catsup instead.

"Coward," she hissed over and over again, all the way to the parking lot.

30

By the time Traveler reached home he felt as if the day's heavy heat was pulling him down with a gravitational force of its own. Mad Bill met him at the door. "As soon as I heard about your father's illness I came to pray with him." He embraced Traveler and dragged him inside. "Charlie's here, too. He brought medicine men with him."

Martin was down on his knees near the fireplace, with Charlie Redwine right beside him. Two Indians wearing headbands, beaded vests, and Levi's appeared to be supervising the prayers from the comfort of the reclining loungers. Both toasted Traveler's arrival with water glasses full of red wine. Their blue denim work shirts had dark, bloodlike stains down the front.

Charlie and Martin had their hands clasped in prayer, but wine was still sloshing in the two glasses that stood next to them on the brick hearth. A fire had been built in the grate, raising the temperature in the room to that of a steam bath. Something had been added to the flames, causing them to burn blue.

"Jesus Christ," Traveler muttered.

"Amen," Bill said, his eyes a mixture of piety and mirth, if Traveler was reading them correctly.

Martin looked up at his son and winked. "One last fling never hurt anybody." His steepled fingers parted and he took his drink.

"I'll bring another glass for Moroni," someone said from the kitchen.

"And then we'll drink the blood of Christ," Charlie said.

"And the blood of our enemy," one of the medicine men added.

The reek of wine, sweat, and marijuana was enough to make Traveler dizzy. He sat on the sofa and closed his eyes. When he opened them a moment later he was looking into the grinning face of Miles Beecham, advising elder to the Council of Seventy, who held wine-filled glasses in either hand.

"Joe Smith and Brig Young both drank at one time," he said, handing one of the tumblers to Traveler. "This just happens to be my time. God loves a repentant sinner. He knows I'll be that much stronger when I return to the Word of Wisdom."

Traveler sipped. The wine tasted vinegary enough for salad dressing.

"If we are to pray as one," Bill said, "we must get in the mood. Tune our minds to the right frequency." He adjusted his summer-weight robe and sat cross-legged at Traveler's feet.

"He means we should all get drunk," Martin said.

"You don't have far to go," Traveler answered.

"Drink up, Mo," Bill advised. "You're going to have to hurry if you want to catch up."

The look on his father's face caused Traveler to drain his glass. The astringent wine puckered his mouth and brought tears to his eyes.

"One refill coming up," Beecham said, and staggered through the doorway leading to the kitchen.

"Bring the goddamned bottle back with you," Charlie shouted, and began passing around joints of marijuana wrapped in aluminum foil. As an ex-smoker of cigarettes Traveler took a pass on the offering; he wasn't about to pick up another bad habit.

By the time Beecham returned from the kitchen with the bottle, there was enough smoke in the living room to rate a warning from the Surgeon General. At the sight of it the Mormon elder took a deep breath, licked his wine-purpled lips, and said, "Joe and Brig smoked, too." The words came out of his mouth slowly, one at a time. "But they eventually found their way to glory."

Charlie snorted. "That's like saying Christ, the Jew, had sense enough to become a Christian."

The medicine men began a rhythmic chanting.

Beecham staggered. Bill rescued the bottle first before providing his shoulder as a prop.

"I thank you," Beecham said, and settled onto the carpet, where he quietly keeled over onto his side and closed his eyes.

"It's time we prayed," Bill said.

The chanting stopped.

Martin held out an empty glass. "I'm not drunk enough."

Bill passed the bottle. It went from hand to hand until every glass but Beecham's had been refilled.

"Down the hatch," Martin said.

"No," Beecham shouted, and sat up suddenly. "I have a toast to propose." He crawled to Martin's side, retrieving the bottle from one of the medicine men along the way, and threw an arm around his friend's shoulder. "To Moroni, the bravest man I ever met." Beecham sounded more sober than before, as if closing his eyes for a few seconds had been as good as a nap.

"My name is Martin," Traveler's father corrected.

"We fought a war together and I can tell you, his friends, that Moroni was a one-man army. No one could shoot like him. He was a natural. Everybody said so right from boot camp. I couldn't hit shit and he didn't even have to aim. Up came that rifle of his and bang, that was it. Five hundred yards, more. It didn't make any difference. If Moroni could see it, he could hit it. He was just as good with a pistol, too.''

Traveler leaned forward; he didn't want to miss a word. Martin never spoke of his service in World War II, though Traveler knew that his father had been one of the state's most decorated heroes.

"Do you remember that sniper in France?" Beecham asked.

"No."

"Near Reims. The bastard who winged me."

"I don't remember a thing."

"You thought I was dead. You went crazy. Took the son of a bitch out when no one else could get near him." Beecham nodded at the memory.

"Are we here to drink or bullshit?" Martin said.

"I never saw anything like it," Beecham went on. "You were a berserker. No other way to explain it. A goddamned killing machine."

"You're drunk," Martin said.

"Am I?" Beecham's looked down at his legs that were stretched out in front of him on the floor. "By God, you're right. The best thing to do is sleep it off."

"We mustn't sleep," Charlie said, gesturing at the medicine men, who quickly nodded agreement. "We must protect Martin from the evil spirits of sickness that steal into our souls at night."

31

The phone woke Traveler from a drugged sleep in which he'd been chasing a shadowy figure that always managed to stay a step ahead. Occasionally the figure stopped. Whenever that happened Traveler's feet became mired in sludge. While he fought to break loose, a woman would appear from behind the figure and write in the air with a sparkler, leaving a clear afterburn: *I am a missionary of the damned.*

"It's Willis," the phone said.

Traveler squinted at the clock face but couldn't bring it into focus.

"Talk to me, Mo."

"Why?" The word came out sounding like a gasp. Traveler swallowed. His throat was on fire. His eyes itched. He couldn't breathe through his nose. He was coming down with a summer cold. "What the hell time is it?"

"Too late for the girl in Sunnyside Park."

Traveler sat up so fast he grew light-headed.

"I've seen her myself, Mo." The sound of ragged breathing came down the line. "What's left of her. It's not Claire."

"Sunnyside Park?" Traveler said stupidly.

"Adjacent to the Veteran's Hospital. You come up Eighth South where it turns into Sunnyside Avenue just above Thirteenth East. As parks go it's not much, some grass, a few trees, a Little League field, a storage building, a parking lot."

"I remember now."

"I want you to meet me there."

"Why?"

"Brother Moyle calls it motivation. He wants you to see what could happen to Claire."

"I haven't forgotten Liberty Park."

"This one's worse."

32

The sound coming from the living room rose and fell like lapping waves. As soon as Traveler stepped through the doorway the tide changed. Snores gave way to coughs and groans. No one had moved since Traveler went to bed. The medicine men were still in their loungers, while Charlie and Bill lay facedown on the carpet, drooling into the nap.

Charlie raised his head, his sluggish tongue trying to wet the lips around it, and stared at Traveler like a stricken animal begging to be put out of its misery. Traveler's head throbbed in sympathy, though he'd limited his wine intake to half that of everyone else.

"Would you like an aspirin?" he asked.

The Indian made a gagging sound and lowered his head back onto the carpet.

Traveler retreated down the short hallway that led to the kitchen where his father was standing at the sink drinking from a cup. Martin seemed unaffected by his indulgence of the night before.

"Good morning," he sang out cheerfully. "Coffee's ready." A whiskey bottle stood on the linoleum countertop next to him.

"In a minute." Traveler retrieved aspirin from the spice cupboard and washed down three of them with lukewarm water. His stomach took their arrival as a personal insult, forcing him to collapse onto a kitchen chair and keep perfectly still while waiting for the nausea to pass.

"Hair of the Indian," Martin said, waving his cup under Traveler's nose. The smell of whiskey was strong enough to make Traveler cringe.

"I've got work to do," he whispered.

"Try vodka then. Nobody will smell it on your breath."

"Just coffee."

Martin ignored the request and began rummaging in the cupboard. Watching his father's methodical search, Traveler realized that it might help to distill his own thoughts if he could discuss the latest killing with Martin. At the same time he didn't want to add to his father's worries.

"By God, I knew it was here," Martin said, and held out an airline minibottle for inspection. He broke the seal and poured the liquor into a coffee cup.

Traveler lowered his forehead onto the cool tabletop and groaned. He'd keep his own council for the time being. He could always talk later, providing Willis Tanner didn't have him arrested for failing to arrive at Sunnyside Park. Viewing another body would be of no help. If there'd been clues to find Tanner would have said so on the phone.

"You wouldn't swallow aspirin when you were a child. I used to mash them up in a spoon and add sugar."

Traveler dry-swallowed at the memory.

"You trusted me then."

"All right." Traveler slowly raised his head. "I'll take your cure."

Martin added an equal amount of coffee to the vodka and presented the cup. "It's drinking temperature right now. If you let it cool off you'll never get it down. It's best not to sip either. Drink it straight down. That's what I did. As you can see it fixed me right up."

"Jesus," Traveler breathed, and gulped the concoction. For a moment he thought he was going to be sick. He gasped. The intake of air helped spread the alcohol's warmth. Gradually his stomach relaxed.

Martin refilled their cups with plain coffee before joining his son at the kitchen table. "After you went to bed Charlie had a vision."

"I heard more chanting."

"He saw the spirit of death."

"You don't believe that," Traveler said.

"Charlie does. I think Bill does, too."

"They were drunk."

"So was I."

"Is there a point to this?"

"I made out my will."

Staring into his father's face, Traveler saw a reflection of his own helplessness. Time and sickness were stealing away what they both valued most.

"Everything is in writing," Martin continued. "All the things we could never say to one another. There are a couple of scrapbooks, too. Believe it or not, your mother put one of them together when I was in the service."

Traveler gulped coffee to keep from saying something that would embarrass them both.

Martin rubbed his glittering eyes. "Moroni's a hell of a name to be saddled with, isn't it?"

Traveler nodded.

"It wasn't so bad for you growing up. You were always big. But me? I was the smallest kid in class. I had to fight the bullies at the beginning of every year. I didn't give a damn if I lost or not, because I wasn't about to let anybody get away with calling me the Angel Moroni."

"I used to think about changing my name," Traveler said.

"To what?"

"Martin, of course."

His father looked away. "Never the last name?"

"I wanted to be your son."

"You are." The words came out in a sudden expulsion of breath.

When Traveler reached for him, his father retreated to the sink where he began running water into his cup. "Since tomorrow's a holiday, I figure Doc Murphy will be calling me sometime today."

"I know."

"He won't be operating on Pioneer Day, not in this state. Not unless it's an emergency."

"He said time wasn't that critical."

"I know what he said, but I don't know what he was thinking." He kept his back to Traveler.

"Do you want me to stay here?"

"Hell, no. I've got enough on my hands with four drunks to nurse back to life. Did the vodka do its job?"

Experimentally Traveler rose to his feet. There was no pain in his head, even when he shook it. But his sore throat persisted, as did the burning sensation in his nose.

"My hangover's gone, but I think I'm coming down with a cold."

His father turned away from the sink. "Here, take my asafetida bag."

"No," Traveler said so adamantly he surprised himself. He wasn't superstitious, but he also wasn't about to take a chance that the old woman's cure might not work.

"Knock wood," Martin said, reading his mind. "The radio says it's going to reach a hundred today. Maybe you can sweat out your cold."

Traveler hugged his father.

"Let go of me," Martin said. "I don't want to catch your damned germs." He broke loose, grabbed up the whiskey bottle, and took a swig, swishing it around like a mouthwash. A wink accompanied his swallow.

33

It was 7 A.M. when Traveler left the house. Sprinklers were on all over the neighborhood, cooling the air beneath a cloudless sky that promised another scorching desert day.

He drove with the windows open, smelling the neighborhoods change, grass giving way to sage as he climbed toward the foothills. By the time he reached The Cove at the base of Mount Olympus pine trees were predominant, their scent carried on down-canyon winds from the Wasatch Mountains.

A folded newspaper, the *Tribune*, lay on the aggregate walkway that led to the Farnsworth house. Traveler picked it up, checking the headline to see if the latest murder had come in under deadline. It hadn't. He carried the paper to the front door and rang the bell. Its ring sounded hollow, as if the house had been abandoned. He rang again and pressed his face against a narrow window that flanked the door. The only thing visible was a marble-topped table in the entrance hall. Several pieces of mail were waiting to be opened.

He started down the side of the house, intending to try the back door, when a neighbor's head appeared over the top of a wooden fence that separated the two properties. It was the same man who'd tried to eavesdrop on Traveler's conversation with Suzanne.

"The bishop is at church," he said, his tone suspicious.

"It's a bit early for services, isn't it?"

"There's no time limit on worshipping God."

Traveler sighed. "I thought I'd knock on the back door."

"We watch out for one another in this neighborhood. That keeps down the crime rate."

"It's important that I speak with Bishop Farnsworth or Suzanne."

"There's no one home." The neighbor pointed toward the road. "My suggestion is that you go back the way you came. Sooner or later you'll see our church's spire."

Mormon churches, Martin once said, were stamped out of a mold somewhere and transported to their locations intact, complete with worshippers. Beauty and grace had been sacrificed to utility, even to fold-away pews and pulpits so the main hall could be converted into a basketball court. Church-sponsored leagues kept God in the minds of the young, or so LDS theory went.

Newell Farnsworth, wearing a baseball hat with the word coach on the front, was supervising from the sidelines, calling occasional fouls, while ten teenagers, skins versus shirts, ran up and down the court.

He spit a whistle from his mouth and shook hands with Traveler. "We practice early to avoid the heat."

The smell inside the church reminded Traveler of high school gym class. He said, "It's your daughter I really want to see."

"I'm sorry. I should have called you with the good news. Everything's all right now. Heber called Suzanne last night."

He glanced furtively toward the far end of the court, where the skins were practicing a four-corner stall, then spoke in a whisper. "He's joined the Saints of the Last Day. There was a time when I would have said he was guilty of heresy. But I'm older now. Nothing seems as certain as it once did."

His shoulders sagged. "I'm disappointed in my uncle, Orson Pack, though. I know in my heart that he's a good man, but he should have told me he was sheltering the boy. It would have saved my daughter a lot of suffering."

Traveler said nothing, unwilling for the moment to stem the flow of words.

Bodies thumped on the wooden floor beneath one of the portable baskets.

"Shit," someone shouted.

Farnsworth blew his whistle. "We'll have no more of that. Bad habits in practice could lose us a league game later on. Now, let's play some good, Christian ball."

The moment the bishop turned his back, one of the skins made an obscene gesture. Two others joined in, causing a gap in defense that led to an easy lay-up.

"Many's the time I've argued with Orson. 'What good are you doing hiding yourselves away in the mountains?' I've asked him over and over. 'You can't spread the word that way.' You know what he said? 'No one wants to listen.' Those were his very words. If he'd been selling polygamy, young bucks would be standing in line to join. But oh, no. The battle cry of the SLDs is no marriage, no progeny. When my daughter heard that Heber had joined them, she was devastated. I tried to tell her that it would pass, that he was too young for that kind of thinking. 'He'll get tired of living with old men,' I said. Old being the key word. For them the world is ending. So it's no wonder they see abstinence as a way of taking everyone else with them."

Farnsworth stopped talking to concentrate on floor play that was threatening to get out of hand. He was about to blow his whistle again when Traveler said, "I'd like to talk to the young man for myself."

The bishop dropped the whistle. "'Keep after him,' I told her. 'He'll weaken.' When I was his age polygamy would have seemed like a dream come true." He tried to grin but produced something closer to a grimace. "Who knows what would have become of me if I'd been able to find enough willing women."

The man's eyes turned inward. Whatever it was he was seeing made him smile. "I've done what I can. Suzanne took my advice. She went off to meet him last night after he called. She wasn't home this morning, so as far as I'm concerned he'll have to marry her now. If the SLDs don't like it, too bad."

"Where did she go?"

"She didn't say."

"Did you talk to him yourself?"

"Yes, I answered the phone."

"And?"

"What do you want from me? I didn't know she was going to spend the night with him, did I?"

"I spoke with Ephraim Moyle yesterday."

Farnsworth caught his breath. Fear competed with the awe in his eyes.

"I'm working for him now," Traveler said, though the words tasted sour in his mouth. "He ordered me to find Heber Armstrong."

The bishop swallowed hard enough to threaten his Adam's apple. "Jack's a good boy."

Traveler grabbed hold of Farnsworth's arm. "Why did you call him Jack?"

"He hates being called Heeb. That's why Suzy nick-named him Jack Armstrong. Like on old-time radio."

34

Traveler called church headquarters from the nearest pay phone and was put right through to Tanner. "Punch up Heber Armstrong on your computer, Willis."

"Why?"

"Just do it."

The clicking sound coming down the line was so loud Traveler suspected that Willis was holding his phone next to the keyboard. "All right, Mo. Now what?"

"Read me what you've got."

"Impossible. That's confidential information."

"I'm working for one of the Twelve Apostles, or have you forgotten?"

"I'll put you on hold."

Before Traveler had time to object the line buzzed momentarily before giving way to a recording of the Tabernacle Choir. One song ended and the *Battle Hymn of the Republic* was beginning when Tanner got back to him. "Exactly what is it you want to know?"

Traveler paused to think that over. Having Jack as a nickname was hardly a motive for murder. On the other hand it was a nasty coincidence.

"I'm not sure. Just start reading."

Biographical data came first. Age, place of birth, date of confirmation as a deacon, church ward, school attendance, both secular and religious, and so on. Nothing took hold in Traveler's mind.

When Tanner paused in his recitation to take a breath, Traveler broke in. "My hunch is that whatever I'm looking for has to be recent. Probably something to do with his mission. What do you have on that?"

"The best person to talk to would be his mission leader. A man named Frederick Samuels."

"Where can I reach him?"

Tanner supplied a London telephone number.

"I'll need your credit card number, Willis."

"You're working for us now. Put it with your expense sheet."

"I'm in a phone booth, for God's sake."

"Don't swear on this line."

"Are you telling me that you're being recorded, Willis?"

"I'm giving you my AT&T number, what else do you want?"

Traveler wrote down the information.

"Wait a couple of minutes before you call, Mo. I'll use our satellite connection to clear you with the London mission."

Three minutes later Samuels was on a line that was clear enough to have been coming from next door. Traveler introduced himself.

"Yes, sir. I was told to stand by. What can I do for you?"

"I'm trying to locate Heber Armstrong."

"I have his file in front of me."

"Why don't we start with your impressions of him first?"

Samuels's sigh was clearly audible. Obviously he would have preferred to confine himself to written facts.

"What comes to mind immediately is that he was a hard worker. A self-starter."

"Were there any problems?"

Another sigh. "One man's problem is another man's religion."

"You know who I'm working for, don't you?"

"Yes, sir."

"Then I'd like you to be more specific."

"I thought of Jack as my friend. Of course, I try to be a friend to all our young men. So when they . . . when the disappearance occurred I did a lot of soul searching. I kept asking myself if I'd been to blame in any way."

"What are you trying to say, Mr. Samuels?"

"A local man, a man named John Sidney, filed a complaint against him. Both Jack and the church, for that matter. Mr. Sidney even went to the police, though God is out of their jurisdiction I'm thankful to say."

"What was the nature of the complaint?"

"The same as it always is. That's why I didn't give it much credence then, or now. Mr. Sidney claimed that Jack, that *we* had stolen his son away from the Church of England. He said we'd all burn in hell for that. He said he'd make sure of it himself. But it was only talk."

35

John Sidney was only too happy to talk. "The boys have gone missing, I understand. Turned their backs on that God of theirs and walked away." His laughter sounded as jarring as his English accent. "I take full credit for it. I'm the one who sent them to hell."

Jesus Christ, Traveler thought. What a dummy he'd been, missing the obvious all along. He hadn't even caught on when he heard the mission leader's slip of the tongue a couple of minutes ago. They, he'd said, indicating more than one. And now Sidney was talking about *them*.

Traveler kept his voice neutral, half afraid the man might hang up. "How did you manage that?"

"I did it for my son. I had to show him that Mormons aren't the saints they pretend to be. Them and their baseball, and their laying on of hands, and their ten percent tithe to God, as if you could buy your way into heaven.

"And all the time they travel around in pairs, like nuns. 'We have been called on two-year missions for God,' they say. 'No women. No impure thoughts.' Bugger that, I say, which is probably what those bloody missionaries do to one another when they can't get women."

"Um-hum," Traveler prompted.

"I hired a whore, paid her in advance, the filthiest one I could find. She smelled something awful when I found her, like she'd had a thousand men and never taken a bath."

Sidney made a grunting sound that was half disgust, half glee. "I took her into my own home and cleaned her up, dressed her like a school girl, and told her to go and watch baseball at the mission and get herself converted. Saints, the Mormons call themselves. Saint Armstrong and Saint Moyle. They took my bait."

Traveler's mouth dropped open.

"They gave her the Word of Wisdom—the same foolishness that my son kept trying to pass onto me—and she went down on her knees and prayed with them. Then she was baptized and told them that she'd fallen in love with the men who'd saved her. The next time she went down on her knees it wasn't to pray. You can bet on that."

A burst of satellite static interrupted.

"Are you still there?" Sidney asked as soon as the line cleared.

"I'm listening," Traveler reassured.

"It turned out I was right about those missionaries. They do everything in pairs, by God. My whore taped everything. I could play it into the phone, if you'd like?"

"I think I'll skip the pornography."

"There's hours of it, an entire night. But that's not what I want you to hear."

The man's demented cackle would have made him a prime suspect had he been in Utah. "Comes the dawn," he said. "That's the part I like best. When our saints woke up as sinners. Of course, she'd slipped them a little something in their Mormon tea. To prime the pump, so to speak."

The high-pitched sound of fast-forwarding tape made Traveler wince.

"Here it is," Sidney said after a moment. "This is what she told them the next morning."

"It's time to pay for your fun, lover boys. The all-night rate is one hundred American dollars apiece. That's a bargain. Otherwise I'd have to charge you by the item. Straight fucks are fifty and you each had two, plus French at twenty-five. I charge both ways no matter who's doing the sucking, so that's another fifty. But bloody hell, I'm sentimental. You two add up to my hundredth fuck this week, so I'll give you a break. One-fifty for the night and we're even.''

The tape gave way to maniacal laughter. ''The clap she gave them for free.''

36

Traveler hung up the phone without saying what he was thinking, that John Sidney had created a monster. It wouldn't have done any good. Judging by the sound of the man, he was consumed by his revenge. Easy revenge at that. Hormones ruled young men of Heber's age. Even the church recognized biological urges. The *Missionary's Hand Book* warned, "Immorality is the most subtle means Satan has to cover a missionary with failure and shame. Missionaries should be on constant guard against familiarity with the opposite sex. Suggestions to protect missionaries from falling into the snares of immorality have been formulated as follows: 1. Never be alone with a woman. 2. Never call a woman by her first name. 3. Do not touch a woman except to shake hands with her."

But that didn't take into account a man like Sidney. Or whores either, for that matter.

Traveler called church headquarters.

"Tell me about Armstrong's mission partner," Traveler demanded the moment Willis Tanner came on the line.

"It's Heber we want you to find."

"Maybe I could do that if you'd be honest with me. Missionaries travel in pairs. Partners become friends. It's inevitable. So my best chance of finding Heber would be to talk to his partner, don't you think?"

"Maybe."

"Then again, maybe you didn't want me coming up with the name Moyle."

Tanner caught his breath.

"Talk to me, goddamn it."

"All right," Tanner said after a moment. "His name is Hyrum Moyle. You can find him with the Saints of the Last Day. When you do, maybe you can talk some sense into him. We can't, that's for sure. He refuses to talk to anybody from the church."

"Cut the theology and tell me how he's related to Ephraim Moyle."

"He isn't."

"I don't believe you."

"Not technically anyway. The apostle has declared his son to be dead."

"No more bullshit, Willis."

The sound of rapid breathing came down the phone line. "From the day Hyrum Moyle became a deacon of the church, he was a marked man, high strung but a brilliant scholar. He was to be the next philosopher of Mormonism. And why not? Many of us feel that his father is the likely successor to Elton Woolley."

"And if young Moyle's heresy among the Saints of the Last Day comes out?"

"We're praying that it doesn't."

"I talked to a man named John Sidney, Willis. I know what happened in England. Prayers won't change that."

"We spoke with him, too. It's too late for Heber Armstrong, we know that. But with God's help Hyrum may come back to us. Right now he is consumed by sin. But he's young. Memory fades. With your help we'll establish communication with Hyrum once again. We'll reinstruct him in the gospel."

"And Heber?"

"God may forgive his sins but we cannot."

"It's a good thing I know you, Willis. Otherwise, I might think you were crazy enough to believe everything you say."

37

It was noon by the time he reached the lodge in the High Uintas. The 10,000-foot climb had left his ears clogged. The siren coming from one of three parked sheriff's cars sounded as if it were being funneled down a long tube. He yawned to relieve the pressure and got out of the car.

A uniformed deputy, one hand on the butt of his revolver, came over to meet him. The man didn't speak until the siren ran down. "Do you have business here, sir?"

Traveler handed him a card.

As soon as the deputy read it his eyes narrowed suspiciously. "How'd you get here so fast?"

"I can't answer that until you tell me what's happened."

"I think you'd better talk to the sheriff." The officer stepped to one side, keeping a safe distance between himself and Traveler, and pointed toward the lodge. "You lead the way, sir."

"Why the siren?" Traveler asked.

"It's a signal to the men we have out searching the area."

"What are they looking for?"

"That's for Sheriff Newhouse to say."

The sheriff met them in the doorway of the lodge. He

was wearing a smile, Levi's, and a heavy plaid shirt. He was tall and lanky, with a leathery face and neck and rough, strong hands that rustled when he rubbed them together. "Well, well. What do we have here, Ned?"

"A private detective."

The smile disappeared. "Who sent for you?"

"I think it might be better if I spoke to you alone."

"Do you now?" The sheriff winked at his deputy. "Back off a ways, Ned. But not too far."

As soon as Ned was out of earshot Traveler spoke quietly. "I'm working for Ephraim Moyle."

The name was better than a bribe. Newhouse's face went though an abrupt metamorphoses, from surprise to awe in the blink of an eye.

"Can you prove it?"

Traveler gave him Willis Tanner's telephone number.

"There's no phone here. I'll have to get myself patched through on the two-way radio."

"Fine by me. But I'd be discreet if I were you."

"Shit," the sheriff said. "A week from now I would have been on vacation." He stalked back toward the highway, using an angry jerk of his thumb to signal Ned to keep an eye on Traveler.

Five minutes later the sheriff returned wearing another smile. Only this one looked sad. "You'd better come on in and listen to what's going on."

Inside the lodge, the Saints of the Last Day were assembled on their log pews, all but Orson Pack and Brother Moab, who were standing slump-shouldered at the front of the room. They were being questioned by two men in dark suits. A third man, a uniformed deputy, was operating a tape recorder. The youngest of the Saints, the one who gathered power from the others to lay healing hands upon Martin, appeared to be missing.

Traveler's entrance brought the conversation to a halt. The sheriff left him standing by the door to hold a whispered conference with the two men in suits, both of whom kept casting skeptical glances in Traveler's direction. While that was going on, Pack and Moab stared at the floor. Finally one of the interrogators nodded and Newhouse came back to lean against the door jamb.

"All right," said the man who'd nodded, "let's go over it again from the beginning."

Moab looked to Pack, whose shoulders slumped even more. When Pack spoke he sounded defeated. "We took in Brother Moyle when he came to us. Brother Armstrong, too. We did so against our better judgment."

He paused to glance briefly at Traveler. "We hid Brother Armstrong from outsiders. That makes us guilty in God's eyes. Guilty of deceit. And guilty of foolishness for believing their pledge. Disease had taught them the evil of fornication, they told us. We reject our bodies, our lusts. And so we welcomed them and prayed with them. We read to them from the good book. 'Those who seek the lusts of the flesh and the things of the world, and do all manner of iniquity; yea, in fine, all those who belong to the kingdom of the devil are they who need fear, and tremble, and quake.'"

Pack fell to his knees and bowed his head. His outstretched hands grappled with one another. "They told us they were brothers. They had been born of a mother named desire and were now corrupted by her. They were sinners come to God. We welcomed them. We believed in their conversion. We raised them on high. We gave them our trust and power to lay on hands. We . . ."

Sheriff Newhouse leaned close and whispered in Traveler's ear. "This Brother Moyle he's talking about, is he a close relative of Ephraim Moyle?"

"Very."

"Shit," he mouthed.

Pack's fingers writhed, opening and closing as if trying to catch hold of the air itself. "I am unclean. God has deserted me. I didn't feel the evil among us until it was too late."

One of the interrogators grunted. "Get to the killing, for God's sake."

"I am speaking for God's sake."

Brother Moab, First Disciple of the Saints of the Last Day, laid a gentle hand upon Pack's shoulder. At the touch, Pack began to shake.

"When they brought the woman here," Moab said, "murder was inevitable. Lust set friend against friend. It was Cain and Abel over again. Brother Armstrong's blood is on our hands. We are as guilty of his murder as Brother Moyle."

38

Traveler went one better than an apostle and evoked the name of the prophet himself, Elton Woolley, in order to escape the red tape. The sheriff didn't like it but knew better than to say so. He let Traveler go with a pass to get by the roadblocks, which both of them knew were already too late. The Saints of the Last Day had been unable to provide information about Hyrum Moyle's car, other than it was blue, or about Claire, either, for that matter. Only one woman had come among them, Suzanne Farnsworth, and that was more than enough as far as they were concerned.

Afternoon was giving way to evening when Traveler reached the city. He was exhausted. The sudden change of altitude and climate had accelerated his head cold. He would have gone home to bed if it hadn't been for something Orson Pack had said. Moyle and Armstrong called themselves brothers. Brothers in trouble might go home. Since Ephraim Moyle was living at the old Hotel Utah to be near his prophet, that left the Armstrong place on Eighth Avenue.

The house looked the same as last time, closed, blinds and curtains drawn against the heat, the Tongan sitting on the front porch. Traveler had his foot on the bottom step of the porch before realizing that something was wrong. There were too many flies, a black swarm of them giving frenzied movement to the Tongan's hands and face.

A surge of adrenaline cleared Traveler's nostrils. His hands were shaking as he drew his pistol and climbed the steps. The wicker chair was soaked in blood, as was the floor beneath it. He waved away enough of the buzzing flies to see that the man's throat had been cut. There were no signs of a struggle. The Tongan must have been caught napping.

Traveler swallowed hard to curb his gag reflex and knocked on the door. When he got no answer, he left the porch and moved cautiously around the side of the house. He was halfway down the driveway, peering into the shady depths of an open garage, when he noticed a rope dangling from the doorway of Heber's boyhood tree house. At the same instant he saw that what he had originally thought to be a clothesline connecting the main house and the elm was, in fact, an electrical cable.

He checked the garage before crossing the backyard's scorched grass to take hold of the rope. He tugged. It felt secure enough, though the prospect of shinnying up twenty feet to the platform started him sweating. He glanced around one more time, took a deep breath, and began to climb.

He saw the woman's feet through the partially open door as soon as he boosted himself onto the wooden deck. Thinking about staked goats, he used his toe to nudge the door all the way open. Suzanne Farnsworth, bound and gagged, was alone in the tree house, which was also a makeshift TV studio, complete with monitors, videotape machines, and what appeared to be computerized editing equipment.

Traveler pulled the rope up after him before going to work on her adhesive bindings. The moment the gag came off she began to cry, softly at first but growing in intensity until sobs convulsed her body. He held her in his arms, making soothing noises until she calmed enough to speak.

"He killed Heber. And the man on the porch. I was there. I watched. He'd taped my mouth and hands. I couldn't do a thing."

Traveler said nothing, preferring to let her tell what happened in her own way.

"Heber confessed everything to me. How he and Hyrum fell into evil with a whore and were diseased. They made a pact then. They called themselves brothers in sin and returned to Salt Lake, where they intended to right the wrongs of the missionary system. Seeing home again brought Heber to his senses. He wanted to get medical treatment, but Hyrum refused. 'Our disease must be expunged by deeds,' he kept saying."

Sobbing took her breath away. Traveler rocked her gently and patiently, until finally she continued.

"Heber was innocent, you understand. Hyrum used him. He needed Heber's TV equipment to make a videotape about murder, though he pretended that it was only play-acting. But Heber started to guess the truth when you first came here looking for him, when his parents drove to the Uintas to tell him about the real murders. Soon after that he contacted me. But it was Hyrum who came to get me, who tied my hands and said he'd kill me if Heber didn't go along with his plans."

She shuddered. "If I hadn't come they wouldn't have fought. Heber didn't have a chance. Not against Hyrum's knife."

Her body stilled momentarily. The tremors returned when she went on. "It's all my fault. I wouldn't sleep with Heber before he left for England. I was afraid. If I got pregnant it would ruin his calling. But I see now that I was wrong. Had I been his lover none of this would have happened."

"You can't be sure of that," Traveler said softly.

"Because of me he's dead."

"It's nothing to do with you."

"The Saints of the Last Day are right. Because of women, evil is perpetuated. Without us God can bring an end to all of Satan's works. It would have been better if Jack had killed me."

"Jack?"

"It was my nickname for Heber. He hated being called Heeb, so I christened him Jack, *Jack Armstrong, the All-American Boy*. But Hyrum took the name for himself. He said it made him one with Heber." She shivered. "Just before he left he said, 'Don't worry. Jack will be back for you later.'"

"Why would he say that?"

"He plans to make one more videotape, of a murder so that everyone can watch him pay his angels' share. He'll have to come here to edit it."

"Who is he going to kill?" Traveler asked, though he already knew the answer.

"A woman named Claire."

"Where is she?"

"Tied up in the trunk of his car."

Traveler broke into the main house where he found Doris and Klaus Armstrong tied to their twin beds. He was still struggling with the tape that bound them when Suzanne blurted out the details of their son's death. After that, he called Willis Tanner again, first to report an end to the would-be Moyle dynasty and then to ask for help.

Tanner promised paramedics for the Armstrongs and the girl, and police and Tongans to scour the city for Hyrum. Traveler did some scouring of his own until exhaustion, abetted by his head cold, forced him home a couple of hours before dawn.

He intended only to shower before resuming the search. But Martin wouldn't hear of it.

"If you don't get some rest, you won't be able to help anyone," he said, while leading Traveler down the hall toward the bedroom. "All I ask is that you lay down and close your eyes for a while. I'll wake you when it's light."

39

Traveler awoke in darkness, momentarily unsure of where he was until he reached out and switched on his bedside lamp. The light, seen through gummy eyelashes, looked distant and muted.

He felt his way into the bathroom quietly, so as not to disturb his father, and eased the door shut behind him. Only then did he run hot water and soak away the mucus residue. When he was finally able to open his eyes all the way, the face he saw in the mirror looked like it belonged in a hospital. His throat was raw, a constant reminder of his father's tumor. Both nostrils were completely plugged.

Coughing, he sat down on the toilet seat and tried to focus on his wristwatch. If everything was in working order, himself and the watch works, dawn was less than an hour away. He got to his feet and went back to bed. But no sooner did his head hit the pillow than he bounced right back up and turned on the light again. He tilted his head first one way and then the other, listening for something, a sound or an idea, he wasn't quite sure, whatever it was that had awakened him in the first place.

A muted explosion, more like a popping sound, made him smile. The neighborhood kids were up already and firing off their fireworks. He knew the feeling well, any excuse to raise hell and make noise. The Fourth of July. The twenty-fourth, today, Pioneer Day. Firecrackers would be exploding all day.

He squinted reassuringly at the calendar thumbtacked to the wall over his childhood desk. A Utah calendar because the twenty-fourth was printed in red. Next to it he'd posted a map of greater Salt Lake, one he studied every so often on the theory that eventually he'd learn all the street names.

A siren, coming up South Temple by the sound of it, prompted another smile. At twelve he'd had a collection of cherry bombs that kept police patrolling the neighborhood for days. He'd eluded them by knowing every nook and cranny in the area.

He left his bed to look for his old escape routes on the map, and that's when it hit him, the idea that had awakened him in the first place.

He opened the center drawer of the desk and sifted through a clutter of old letters, photographs, pencils, and paper clips until he found a yellow day-glow marking pen. Uncapping it, he started circling the murder scenes, beginning with Jordon Park and working his way toward the last one, Sunnyside.

"Jesus Christ," he muttered, and connected the circles with a broad yellow line. It was like an arrow pointing at Pioneer Trail State Park, the hallowed Mormon ground where Brigham Young had said, "This is the place." The very reason behind today's celebration.

What better time and place for a disillusioned missionary to make an ultimate statement of sacrilege? To pay his tithe in blood. Claire's blood.

Traveler snatched up the phone, intending to call the police. He'd dialed two digits before deciding on a change of tactics. When it came to protecting church interests, the police would be certain to overreact. Willis Tanner would, too, for that matter. But Traveler had no choice. He had to stick with the church on this one. And who knew? When dealing with missionaries, even disenchanted ones, he might need an expert on theology.

He dialed Tanner's home number from memory. The man sounded wide awake despite the hour.

"Meet me at Pioneer Park," Traveler told him without preamble.

"Now?"

"I'll be parked on the side of the road, say a quarter of a mile from the entrance."

"I know you, Mo. You've come up with something."

"I'm working for your apostle," Traveler reminded him. "I'm certain he'd want you to cooperate."

Tanner made a grumbling noise that sounded vaguely obscene. "How soon?"

"Before the sun comes up."

Traveler was checking his .45, one of Martin's mementoes from the war, when his father walked into the sun room where they kept their guns.

"What's wrong, son?"

Without looking up from the ammunition clips he was loading, Traveler quickly explained the situation, that he was on his way to find Claire, who was in the hands of a killer.

Martin rubbed his throat as he stared at the pistol. For years he'd been refusing to handle cases that required him to carry a firearm.

"I'm going with you," he said quietly.

Traveler recognized the tone. Arguing would be useless, even if he did have the time to waste.

His father crossed to the gun cabinet and took out the twin to his son's .45. Traveler tossed him a loaded clip, which Martin snapped into place. He cocked the weapon, checking its mechanism.

"I don't want you doing something stupid," Traveler said.

"Like what?"

"Like taking the easy way out."

"If this is cancer," Martin said, again massaging his throat, "I don't intend to waste away. But I won't pull the plug without fair warning, either."

"All I'm asking is that you be careful. This bastard thinks he's the reincarnation of Jack the Ripper."

"Will you drive or should I?"

40

The barrier leading to Pioneer Park was still in place when they arrived. But the padlock had been broken. There was no sign of Willis Tanner.

"I think we'd better wait for him," Martin said.

In the distance the floodlit monument reminded Traveler of a monolithic tombstone, ablaze against the blackness of the Wasatch Mountains.

"The sun will be coming up soon," Traveler said. Even as he spoke the eastern sky seemed to grow perceptibly lighter, outlining the jagged peaks. "He'll be able to see us coming if we don't hurry."

"Shit," his father murmured. "Let's go, then."

Traveler led the way into the park, his breath clouding the chill morning air. He kept to the asphalt road and moved as quietly as possible. His nose had cleared enough for him to identify the smell of pine and sage that was blowing down from the mountains.

Every so often he paused to listen, but all he could hear was his father's labored breathing, made worse by the tumor that was restricting the passage of air in his throat.

Traveler stopped when they were about a hundred yards from the monument. "Stay here," he whispered. "There will be less noise if I go on alone."

Martin sighed. "It's hell to get old."

Traveler rechecked the .45 before tucking it into the belt at the small of his back. His father kept his own pistol holstered beneath his armpit.

"Be careful," Martin said.

Traveler nodded and moved off without a word. Approaching the monument, a stone pillar that rose from two massive granite wings, he had the feeling that he was slipping back in time. At any moment Brigham Young's bronze likeness would step down from his perch, pronounce this his promised land, and lead them all to glory.

The sound of a mere mortal disappointed him. "We've been waiting for you," it sang out.

Traveler looked to the pinnacle, to Brigham. But the prophet hadn't moved. Nor had his two bronze companions. But one of the shadowy figures lower down, on a flanking wing, broke from the surrounding group of statuary to wave. The base of the wing on which he stood must have been twenty feet off the ground, impossible to scale without a ladder or rope.

"Jack's the name," came a shout. "God promised to send me an angel. And here you are, Moroni himself."

Traveler moved forward cautiously. He didn't see Claire until he reached the visitor's sidewalk near the monument's base. She was tied in among the cluster of statues from which Hyrum Moyle had emerged.

Still in shadow, Moyle raised his arms toward heaven. The movement was enough to bring his face into the bright beam of a floodlight. It was the bearded young man who'd laid healing hands on Martin during their visit to the Saints of the Last Day.

"Look, Claire," he said. "Moroni has come to collect his angels' share in person."

The first shaft of sunlight slid between the peaks of the Wasatch Mountains. It caught the knife in Moyle's hand and the video camera that was standing on a tripod a few feet away.

"Angels don't need guns," he said to Traveler. The blade touched Claire's throat. "Now get rid of it."

He couldn't possibly see the pistol, Traveler reasoned, but didn't dare argue. Using fingertips only, he drew his pistol and dropped it. Its loss made him feel useless. A real angel would be needed to leap the twenty feet of granite that separated him from Claire.

"I know what happened in England," Traveler said. "I can understand how you must feel, Hyrum."

"Hyrum is diseased. I'm Jack. I won't be Hyrum again until I've cleansed myself with blood."

He entwined the fingers of his free hand in Claire's hair, now highlighted by the rising sun.

"For God's sake," Traveler shouted. "A little antibiotic and you'll be—"

"Man cannot cure what God has intended. Hyrum and I have been chosen to expose the church and its missionaries."

Rising panic had Traveler short of breath. He peered from side to side without moving his head. Were there toeholds among the granite blocks that formed the monument's base? If so, how long would it take him to reach the man? A lifetime, he decided. Claire's lifetime.

"I'm not a member of the church," Traveler said. Anything to forestall the man. "So don't expect me to believe in crusades."

"God brought you here, Moroni. It was part of His plan that Suzanne should glimpse Jack outside the ZCMI. 'Hire an angel to find him,' God told her. And now you're here, the Angel Moroni himself to witness this, my final tithing."

He kicked a rope ladder over the side of the granite slab. "The camera is running on remote control, taping everything that happens. You may come up if you'd like, but only after her blood has cleansed me."

Traveler didn't move.

"We've been watching you, Jack and I. We were there when Claire came to see you." He jerked Claire's head back, exposing the flesh of her neck. "She's like all the others. She, too, offered to sleep with me, to infect me anew with the disease of corruption."

He laughed, a sound that scraped Traveler's spine. "We stand no chance against them, you know. Joe Smith realized that when he sent out his first missionary. He knew we'd be tempted. It was his plan. He and his brother, Satan."

His knife left her throat to slash the air around her groin. "*The Book of Mormon* teaches us that the first Masonic lodge was organized by the Devil to turn people away from God. Joe Smith was a Mason, you remember. That's how I recognized him as Satan's disciple."

"Jesus," Traveler murmured to himself. He'd heard it all before, the wild rumors that Mormon-baiters like Mad Bill loved to spread. Until now Traveler had never known anyone to take them seriously.

"Masons!" the man shouted, and pointed in the direction of the parking lot behind Traveler.

Traveler spun around. The sun had cleared the peaks of the Wasatch and caught Willis Tanner creeping forward with four Tongans. Once revealed, they stopped dead in their tracks. Martin was visible, too, though he'd stayed where Traveler had left him, well out of harm's way.

"Goddamn it, Willis," Traveler shouted in frustration. "Don't move."

Tanner's only response was to stare up at the monument.

"Satan's acolyte may stay," Moyle said. "The rest must go."

"He means your bodyguards, Willis. Send them away. *Now.*"

Traveler's tone of voice jarred Tanner into action. "Wait with the old man," he called loudly to his companions. Once they were on their way, he came forward to stand beside Traveler.

"God has answered my prayers," Moyle said. "Witnesses are present. Into their hands I will deliver my angels' share, that no more innocents will be sent into temptation. Your testimony will raise the Saints of the Last Day to glory."

"There will be no publicity," Tanner said. His voice sounded calm, a far cry from the look in his eye.

Moyle manipulated Claire's head in a gesture that denied the statement.

"No one will ever know what happens here," Tanner added.

"For God's sake," Traveler murmured. "Don't provoke him."

The man pointed the knife in Martin's direction. "I want another witness. The senior Angel Moroni."

Traveler half turned and beckoned to his father. Martin said something to the Tongans before moving toward the monument. The Tongans stayed put.

"Moroni Traveler and son know better than to testify against the church," Tanner said.

"Is that right, my angel?"

"I came here because of Claire," Traveler answered. "Give her to me and I'll be your witness. My father, too."

"I can only give you her blood."

"You've paid enough tithe." Traveler sneaked a look at the .45 he'd tossed aside. It was a yard away, an insane distance if he were to attempt to scoop it up and fire before Moyle could cut Claire's throat.

"Kick the gun farther off or I'll kill her now," the man said as if reading Traveler's mind.

Traveler skidded the .45 across the pavement toward his father. It fell far short of Martin, who was still twenty yards away.

"My angel needs a miracle, not an old man," Moyle said, and pressed the tip of his knife against the skin beneath Claire's chin. "I can pay my tithe long before the senior angel reaches your gun."

Moyle turned his head as if to kiss Claire good-bye.

Out of the corner of his eye Traveler saw Martin draw

his own .45. Traveler's mouth was opening in protest even as the pistol came up. No aiming. Just one smooth motion and then the explosion. The impact of the slug hurled Moyle from the monument. For Traveler it would have been an impossible shot.

Martin came forward, shaking his head in bewilderment, the butt of the gun held out toward his son. "That's why I'm afraid to carry one of these damned things."

41

Claire's tears were gone but she refused to let go of Traveler as they sat in the backseat of the church limousine and waited for the police to complete their examination of the body. A few feet away Martin was watching them through the windshield. Behind him stood Tanner, surrounded by his Tongans.

"You rescued me just as I always wanted," she said softly. Her head was on his shoulder, her lips within inches of his ear. "You proved your love."

He wanted her more than ever.

She kissed his cheek. "Come home with me, Moroni, so I can reward you properly."

A part of him, he realized, still loved her. The part he didn't trust.

Her hands released their hold on his clothing to roam his body. He captured them before they got too far.

"Make love to me, Moroni." Her mouth found his. Her tongue scalded his senses.

He broke free of her and got out of the car. It was one of the hardest things he'd ever done.

"You love me," she said breathlessly. "I know you do."

He closed the door and leaned against it. She lowered the window and offered her lips again. "The least you can do is kiss me good-bye."

He didn't dare.

"I'm sorry, Claire."

"Is that all you have to say, you bastard?"

He started to turn away.

"Remember those two men who attacked you in the parking lot?"

Her question held him.

"Blackie and Lamar. They're friends of mine. I watched it all from across the street."

He swallowed the emotion that was about to spill out and joined his father.

"I've had it," Martin said immediately. "I'm retiring."

"You're in shock, Dad. I know how you feel."

"I doubt that."

"I've killed, too."

Martin breathed in and out quickly. "There are some things about me, son, that I've never told you."

"The war?"

His father nodded.

"Let's go home, Dad."

"No, you don't," Willis Tanner said, stepping between them. "I've got to talk to you, Mo. Privately." He waved the briefcase in his hand.

"Go ahead, son. Get it over with."

With Traveler in tow, Tanner threaded his way across a parking lot full of police cars, enough to form a Pioneer Days parade of their own. He didn't stop until he reached a park bench far enough away to be out of anyone's earshot. There they sat side by side, with Tanner balancing the square-cornered case on his lap in order to open it. Inside was a telephone that looked complicated enough to be a computer.

"It has a built-in scrambler," he explained. "That way our conversations can't be monitored."

"What's the point, Willis?"

Ignoring the question, Tanner held the handset against his ear and began punching in numbers. "Someone wants to speak to you."

"Who?" Traveler sounded as weary as he felt.

Tanner signaled for silence before pressing a palm against his unoccupied ear to block out background noise that was coming from police and Tongans alike.

"Sir, it's Willis Tanner. Yes, sir. He's here with me now. We're on scramble."

He handed the phone to Traveler and mouthed, "It's the prophet."

"Mr. Traveler, this is Elton Woolley."

Despite everything, death, Claire, Martin's illness, even his own head cold, Traveler felt a sense of awe. As president of the church, its living prophet, Woolley spoke for God to millions of believers.

"I'm standing on the balcony of my penthouse," the prophet said.

Traveler envisioned the top floor of the old Hotel Utah, directly across the street from the temple.

"Do you know what I see?"

Traveler waited. No answer was expected of him.

"I see Brigham Young's city, his dream. Did you know that he told us to keep the center of each block open, because some day we'd need that space to park wagons. Had we listened to him then, our streets wouldn't be clogged with automobiles today. But that's the price we pay for growth. And grow we must. That's why we send out missionaries. To spread God's word and strengthen His church. You understand that, don't you, Moroni?"

Though surprised by the use of his first name, Traveler managed to say, "I'm not sure."

"You were born here in Zion," Woolley continued. "And now that we are under attack we call upon you, our son, to use restraint. Forget what you have seen and heard."

"My memory isn't what it used to be."

"I like the sound of that."

"These days I find that I have trouble concentrating on two things at once. If I had Maria Gomez's work permit on my mind, for instance, one that would allow her to stay in this country legally, everything else would go right out of my head."

"Consider it done."

"Thank you."

"Oh, there's one more thing. I keep track of all my Moronis, whether they call themselves Martin or not."

Traveler caught his breath.

"You'll find Dr. Murphy waiting for you at home. He has some good news."